Murder With a Drizzle of Syrup

An Ivy Clark Mystery

Kristy T Dixon

Murder With a Drizzle of Syrup (An Ivy Clark Mystery, book 5)

Copyright © 2025 by Kristy T Dixon

Book Cover by Mariah Sinclair

Edited by Jenny Sims

1st edition 2025

ISBN 978-1-960841-41-4 ebook

ISBN 978-1-960841-42-1 paperback

To Shannon Draper

Chapter 1

The platter full of chocolate chip cookies looked fantastic. I moved it from the diner's kitchen to our exclusive party room with caution. The diner had recently been expanded, and this was the first time the room had been scheduled.

The Muddy Creek book club sat around a large table, talking and sipping their hot chocolate. I knew most of them because they attended my Zumba classes. I'd begun teaching Zumba again, but only once a week. With the freezing temperatures, getting people to come out was hard.

"Cookies!" I said, placing them in the middle of the table.

"Thanks, Ivy," Barbra said, pushing her purple hair over her shoulder. "This room is delightful. Much better than discussing books with all the other people in the diner staring at us."

"If you didn't all talk so loud, it wouldn't be a problem," Barbra's friend Opal said.

Barbra laughed. "I can't deny that. We do get loud. Why don't you join us, Ivy? I know it looks like the retirement club in here, but you might enjoy it."

I smiled. I would love to join a book club, but I didn't have time. "Thanks, but I need to make sure things are running smoothly in the kitchen."

Boyd Webster winked at me and rubbed his goatee. "What Ivy really means is, she can't see the front door from this room, and she might miss Sheriff Jett coming in." The others laughed, and I rolled my eyes.

"She looks guilty to me," Barbra said.

"You guys are impossible," I said, turning to the door. "Can I get you all anything else?"

"Nope," Barbra said. "We'll holler if we need you."

I returned to the kitchen and glanced through the long window connecting the kitchen and dining area. No one had come in while I was gone. Shaking my head, I grabbed my mixing bowl. I needed to stop looking out that window. It just made me antsy.

"He's busy with a bunch of things," José, my head cook and the manager of my diner, said. "He'll be back."

I gave a short laugh. "What are you talking about, José?"

"I know you're looking for Jett. He hasn't been around a lot because he's been out of town with all the trials he has to testify in. Besides that, he has a mountain of paperwork."

"I know that." Hooking the bowl to the mixer, I tried to hold in a sigh. Jett was busy, but he had a phone, didn't he? He'd only given short answers the few times I'd texted him in the past few weeks. I'd thought our relationship had changed, but I must have been wrong.

"Did you know Livy Smith is back?" Carrie, one of the cooks, asked.

I frowned and turned to her. "No, why? The semester isn't over yet." Livy had been one of my servers until she'd gone off to college.

"Did you hear about that group of college dropouts camping outside town?"

My eyes narrowed. "Please tell me she isn't part of that."

Carrie nodded. "She is. They're staying in Livy's family's cornfield."

I took a deep breath. Livy had been so excited about college. I wondered what had changed. She hadn't been gone for more than a couple of months. I'd only talked to her once since she left, but she said she enjoyed it.

"I should go talk to her," I said. "Who camps in the snow? That's crazy."

"They've dug a bunch of snow caves," José said. "Jett told them it's too cold to stay out, but they didn't seem to care. He said he couldn't do anything because they weren't breaking any laws."

"When did you talk to Jett about it?" I asked.

"Two days ago."

I tried not to look distressed. Jett hadn't talked to me in over a week. I hadn't even seen him. I didn't know why I was stressed. We'd never come to any understanding. Sure, he'd kissed me a few times and hinted at some things, but he'd never even taken me on a date—unless you counted sneaking around spying on people as dates. We'd done that a few times. I thought about the time we'd been hiding in a closet and ended up kissing. That might count.

"Do you need me?" I asked José.

"No, I think we're good."

"I'll be back." I hurried out of the kitchen, through the dining area, and up the stairs to my living quarters. Creepers meowed at me from my bed, and I picked him up and cuddled him. I opened the door that led to my new living room. I smiled and flipped on the electric fireplace, then sat down on my overstuffed recliner.

I loved my new area. I'd had the contractors add a living room, small kitchen, bedroom, and bathroom. It was nice to feel like I had an actual place and not just a room above the diner. Creepers curled up in my lap and yawned.

I rubbed my hand over Creepers's soft gray fur. I still hadn't shown Jett all the new space up here. My mouth turned down. He might not care. He'd seemed excited about it while it was being built, but now that it was finished, he hadn't made an effort to come by.

"Why am I like this?" I asked Creepers. "I really thought Jett liked me. I think he's trying to politely phase me out. If he can take time to talk to José, I would think he could talk to me."

Creepers meowed and swatted at my arm. "I know, I'm crazy," I said, but I secretly wondered if Deputy Ledford was influencing Jett. Ledford had told me I was hurting Jett's image. Jett told me it wasn't true, but I wondered if he'd thought about it some more and changed his mind. It was an election year, and someone was running against him this time. It wasn't like last time when he'd won by default.

My phone rang, and I pulled it from my pocket. My heart sped up when I saw Jett's name. I clicked the button and held it to my ear. "Hello?"

"Hey, Ivy. It's Jett."

"Hi."

"Did José tell you about Livy?"

"Yes."

"I'm a little nervous about that group. Ledford's keeping an eye on them, but if you see Livy, can you try to talk some sense into her?"

"Sure. About dropping out of school or living in an empty cornfield?"

"Both."

"Alright."

"Thanks. I don't want this turning into some hippie commune or something. I didn't have time to say too much to her when I was there. Everything's been so busy lately."

"Yeah, we haven't seen you a lot." I realized I was still wearing my hairnet, so I quickly pulled it from my head and let my long, blond hair fall down. Not that Jett could see me through the phone anyway.

"I can't believe how many trials are all happening close together. It's good that Ledford's there to hold things together."

Deputy Ledford wasn't the most pleasant of my acquaintances, but I was glad Jett had some help.

"Are you in Wichita?" I asked.

"Yes. It's been brutal."

"I'm sorry."

"It's fine, just busy. I have to run. I'll talk to you later."

"Alright, see you."

"Hopefully soon. Bye."

I hung up and leaned against the chair. He'd seemed normal enough. I ran my hand over Creepers and sighed as I analyzed the conversation. It had been the longest conversation I'd had with him in a few weeks.

"This is no good," I told Creepers. "If I sit up here, I'm going to get depressed. I put Creepers on the chair and went back to the diner. Right as I walked into the dining area, the door opened, and a small group came in. I recognized Livy's bright red hair. That was convenient. Now I wouldn't have to search for her.

"Hey, Ivy!" she said, hurrying over to me. She gave me a hug, and I patted her back.

"It's good to see you," I said. It really was. Livy had been our best server.

"Come meet my friends," she said, pulling me over to the group.

"Everyone, this is Ivy. She owns Sue's Diner."

A boy about twenty with black hair and deep brown eyes held out his hand. "Livy's been talking this place up forever. I'm Carlos Hernandez."

"Nice to meet you," I said.

Livy pointed at the others. "This is Hannah." She pointed at a blond girl who was only as tall as Livy's shoulder. Hannah nodded and looked bored. "Then this is Noah Cutler and Jacob McComb." They both shook my hand. The boys had similar hairstyles and features, which would make them hard to tell apart.

"Let me get you a table," I said, leading them to a booth. They all scooted in, and Noah placed his arm over Hannah's shoulders. I was surprised Jacob had sat next to Hannah. I wouldn't want to be that close to an obvious couple. Carlos put his arm over Livy, and I understood. Jacob was the only one not in a relationship. He also looked a little older than the others.

"I'll send one of the servers right over," I said, turning and pointing them out to Elle. Elle pulled her little black braids into a ponytail and hurried over with her notepad, and I went into the kitchen. I would talk to Livy later when she wasn't in front of her friends.

"Livy's here," I said. José and Carrie nodded, and Anton looked over from where he was putting on his apron. "She brought some friends."

Anton walked over and looked out the window and into the dining area. "Looks like she has a boyfriend."

I shrugged. "Maybe. She didn't say."

Anton's brows came together, and he frowned.

"Is anything wrong?" I asked.

He shook his head. "No. I just think it's weird they're living out in a cornfield. I doubt it's safe. Not in this temperature. Can I go say hello before I start?"

"Sure."

Anton rushed from the kitchen, then went over and began talking to Livy and her friends.

Carrie tilted her head. "Does Anton like Livy?"

José looked up from the burger he was cooking. "Not that I know of. They got along fine when she worked here but didn't seem overly friendly."

"Jett called me," I said. "He wants me to talk to Livy."

Carrie nodded. "Someone needs to. I'm surprised her parents are letting them all live on their land."

José nodded. "They probably figure it's better to let them stay and know where she is."

I heard the bell over the door and peeked through the window. It was another group of young people I didn't recognize. There were about ten of them, and they were all talking and laughing. I saw Elle hurry over to them.

"How many people are living in the cornfield?" I asked.

"Jett said there were about fifteen," José said.

"I think they must all be here."

Elle had them all seated, and Trina went over to help take the orders.

José's mouth turned down. "We better tell Elle and Trina to watch them closely. They're the kind that might run out without paying."

Anton came back in and grabbed his hairnet. "I can't believe Livy's hanging out with that group. They're all a little rude, especially the guy with brown hair."

I looked at the group from the window. "I think his name is Jacob."

"You're already memorizing their names?" Anton asked, grinning.

I smiled. "You never know when you might need information."

"So long as no bodies turn up, I'm good.

"We haven't had one of those in a while," José said."

I yawned. "And it's a good thing. It sounds like Jett is busy enough without adding anything to his plate."

Anton gave me a teasing smile. "And if you have to solve a case when Jett's gone, you'll have to work with Ledford."

I laughed. "Not going to happen. I'm pretty sure Ledford hates me."

José put the burger on a bun. "That's because Jett's solved more cases with you than with him. He's jealous."

Even though my phone call with Jett had been low-key, I still felt better than I had before. He had said he hoped to see me soon. I went into the party room to check on the book club.

"Boyd, you didn't read the book!" Barbra accused.

Boyd swallowed his cookie. "What do you mean?"

"You're only adding things from the beginning of the chapters. You skimmed it."

Boyd smiled and shrugged. "You got me."

Opal patted her short gray hair. "If you want to come to book club, read the books."

I hid a smile. Boyd probably only came to talk to all the ladies and eat cookies. He had a huge crush on Barbra, and for being seventy, he was moving really slow.

"Well, why don't we read something worth reading?" Boyd asked.

Opal crossed her arms. "We voted. You missed that meeting, so you can't blame us. We did tell you."

"I won't miss the next one," Boyd muttered. "You would think *The Lord of the Rings* would have been voted in."

I hope this didn't turn into another bingo night. Jett had helped this same group and ended up with a black eye.

"No one wants to read that," a woman named Holly said. "It's boring."

"And this isn't?" Boyd asked, gesturing at his book on the table. "When they speak in British, I can't follow."

Opal let out the longest sigh I'd ever heard. "That is because you aren't cultured. British English is much more sophisticated. And the language is called English, not British."

"I bet you're going to make us watch the movie when it's over."

"We're going to watch the miniseries," Barbra said. "Everyone here is dying to get together and drool over Colin Firth."

"Not everyone," he muttered. "I'm guessing he's an actor from the United Kingdom?"

"Yes, and he's adorable," Barbra said.

Opal's mouth turned down. "He's too young for you."

Barbra rolled her eyes. "That's why I said adorable and not attractive."

"Well, I think he's attractive," Holly said.

"But you said you want to drool over him," Opal accused Barbra.

"Don't be a prude, Opal. You're too old to miss out on the small joys in life."

"Do you all need anything?" I asked, hiding a smile.

No one answered. They just went back to their disagreement. I returned to the kitchen and could hear arguing in the dining area. I went over to Livy's table. Elle stood there looking like she wanted to escape, and Jacob and Noah were glaring at each other.

I motioned for Elle to leave, and she scurried away, mouthing, "Thank you."

"I paid last time," Noah said.

"Maybe we should always pay for ourselves," Livy suggested.

"No," Jacob said. "That's not how our group works. We all take care of each other, so Noah pays. He has the most."

"That doesn't seem right," Carlos argued.

Jacob glared. "Are you challenging me?" Carlos shook his head. "Good."

Noah shook his sandy-brown hair and scowled. "I'll pay."

"You shouldn't have to pay," Hannah said. "You always pay."

"I can split the check," I offered.

"No," Jacob said. "Noah pays." His eyes narrowed as he glared at everyone at the table. "He pays for everyone at those tables, too." He pointed at the other two tables of young people.

"You're such a bully," Hannah said.

Noah glanced at her. "No, it's fine. I have plenty." He handed me the bill and his debit card.

"Not forever," Hannah said.

Jacob stood and left the diner.

Livy tried to hand Noah some money, but he wouldn't take it. I was uncomfortable butting in since I didn't know the group. They were going to have to figure this out on their own. I returned to the kitchen and handed the card and bill to Elle. This wasn't good. It looked like Jacob had made himself the ruler of the college dropouts.

Chapter 2

Pulling my pink beanie lower over my forehead, I shivered. "Are you sure we should start this in the winter?" I asked José. "Running seems like something you should avoid when it's snowy." It was still dark, and my eyes didn't want to focus.

"If you want to get good at running, it can't be a seasonal thing."

I looked at the mostly clear sidewalk and nodded. José runs the occasional marathon, so trusting him to know what to do was probably smart. I could imagine myself slipping on my head.

"How do you keep yourself from falling?"

"Run carefully."

"Have you ever fallen on your backside?"

"Sure. A few times."

I hugged myself. My jacket wasn't blocking the wind. "Don't you worry about people seeing you?"

He laughed. "I run when it's dark."

"I'm not sure this is a good idea."

José tilted his head and studied me. "How many times have you wished you were better at running in the past year?"

"A lot."

"So are we going to do this?"

I took a deep breath, and my nose hurt from the cold air. "Okay."

"We're going to run for one minute, then walk for a minute. Ready?"

"Ready."

José began running, and I followed him down the sidewalk. He told me he usually ran down the street, but I worried about that. With each thud my new running shoes made against the ground, I counted. When I got to sixty, I expected José to stop, but he didn't. He must be going for actual seconds, not just steps.

When I got to one hundred and twenty, he stopped, and we walked briskly. After what seemed like less than a minute, he began running again. I kept up, but I was sure he was going slow for me.

We did this a few times, and I was breathing hard and getting a stitch in my side. When we walked, I turned to

José. "I'm going to drop any second. I should be in better shape from all the Zumba."

"Every exercise is different. Just because you can do one doesn't mean you can do another without training."

"How long will it take before I'm used to it?"

"Depends."

"I don't think I can go any farther."

José glanced at me. "One more minute of running and one more walking." He didn't wait for an answer before he started running again. I took a shaky breath and followed. When he finally stopped, I put a hand to my side. We hadn't been at this long, and I was sweating even in the cold.

I spotted one of Livy's friends. I thought his name was Noah. He stood by the hardware store, talking to someone I didn't know. The man was in his early forties with a cowboy hat and held a backpack with a cartoon character on the front. He handed the pack to Noah, and they shook hands. When the man saw me watching, he turned and disappeared behind the store. I didn't feel like analyzing it.

"I don't know how you do this," I said.

José grinned. "I don't. I usually run ten miles."

"That's insane."

"When you get to be my age, you need to stay in shape."

"I can't believe I'm getting outrun by—"

"An old guy?" He laughed. "I can outrun anyone in Muddy Creek."

"Come to my Zumba class, and I'll see what you've got."

"No way. You can't pay me enough to go work out with that group. Running is how I deal with stress. Exercising with Barbra and Boyd wouldn't do much for my mental state."

"It's actually pretty entertaining. I think I'm the only person under sixty, and those people are determined."

"Do they complain as much as you do about running?"

I grinned. "Only Opal."

"Opal complains about everything. Do you want to race back?"

I groaned. "Not a chance."

He laughed. "Then I'm going to run a few miles. I'll see you in an hour." José ran in the opposite direction, and I trudged to the diner.

Livy popped into my mind. I had trouble sleeping last night because of her. She needed to get away from those people, especially that Jacob. I didn't like the way he was controlling people. Someone needed to do something, but with Jett gone, I wasn't sure who. I rolled my eyes. That was a stupid thought. I knew I was going to interfere. I was starting to think my life revolved around butting into other people's business.

After my shower, I could hear music coming from down-stairs. I hurried to get dressed and clomped down the stairs to the diner. José stood by the jukebox smiling while Elvis Presley played.

"You fixed it?" I asked, walking over to the ancient machine. The jukebox had never worked as far as my memory went. Gramma Sue used to talk about how fun it had been when she first got it.

"Yep," José said with a grin. "It only took months and several YouTube tutorials."

"That's so amazing!"

"We might want to play it without charging for a while, just so people know it works."

"I'm so excited," I said, running my hand over the top.

"You say that now, but just wait until you get someone who comes in and plays the same annoying song over and over."

I looked at the song options and smiled. Since it hadn't worked, I'd never paid attention to the songs. I've always loved listening to music from before my time. Something about it excited me and made me want to dance.

"When have you worked on this? I've never seen you."

"I mess around with it before you come down in the morning."

The front door opened, and Boyd came in. "The jukebox works! That thing hasn't worked in forty years!"

"You remember it working?" I asked.

"Sure. It wasn't that long ago."

I smiled. "I wasn't even born."

"Well, you aren't that old." Boyd came over and stared inside. "Does it still cost a nickel?"

"It does unless we can figure out how to change it," José said.

I rubbed my lip. "Let's leave it. I don't see any reason to overcharge people to hear music."

The song ended, and Boyd reached into his pocket. He pulled out his wallet and grabbed a nickel. He slipped it in the slot and fiddled around with the machine. Herman's Hermits blasted "I'm Henry VIII, I Am" across the diner.

"This is my favorite," Boyd said. "I used to play this over and over until your grandma Sue wanted to kick me out."

José moaned. "I knew it. We need to set rules now. Boyd can only choose one song a day."

Boyd chuckled and patted his wallet. "My nickels don't agree with that."

"Fine, but you can't listen to the same song over and over."

"I'll think about it."

"At least it's a fun song," I said.

José shook his head. "It won't be after you've heard it sixty times in one day."

Boyd rubbed his goatee. "I'll have to go into Wichita to get more nickels."

"I'm going to get the kitchen ready," José said. "And I might order some earplugs."

Boyd laughed. "This is going to be fun."

I cocked my head. "What? Bothering José?"

He winked. "Maybe a little. What are friends for if you can't drive them mad every now and again?"

Now that I knew what was happening downstairs, I went back up to ensure Creepers had what he needed for the day. I grabbed a clean water dish and filled his food bowl. When he heard me, he came lazily over and rubbed against my leg.

"Hungry?" I rubbed his back and sat down while he ate. José wouldn't need me in the kitchen until later. "What are we going to do about those friends of Livys?"

Creepers ignored me and kept eating. His collar was beginning to look faded. I should probably get him a new one. "Do you want a new collar? I bet I could get Boyd to put it on you." I'm not good at putting collars on cats. Creepers doesn't seem to mind his collar, but he won't hold still when I put it on. He's a lot better behaved for Boyd.

Once his dish was empty, Creepers yawned and ran back to my room. I stood and washed my hands. "It must be nice to sleep whenever you want to," I called to him. He meowed, and I smiled. Life was so much better when you had a cat.

Chapter 3

Deputy Ledford stared at me as I stood in front of his desk. I couldn't believe I was here to talk to him. I wanted to call Jett, but he couldn't do anything from Wichita. That only left Ledford. I'd waited until the next day so I had time to think it through.

"Sheriff Malone isn't here," Ledford said, his expression blank.

"I know. I just wanted to talk to you about the college students living outside town."

He sighed and rubbed his mustache. "What about them?"

"There's a guy living there named Jacob. I think he might be taking advantage of the others."

Ledford steepled his fingers and looked at me. "How so?"

"I think he's forcing some of them to give him money or at least pay for all his stuff. He made one guy pay for fifteen people's food at the diner. They're probably scared to go against him."

Ledford took a deep breath through his nose. "That sounds typical for a group like that."

"Can't you do something about it?"

"Not unless he does something illegal."

"Isn't it illegal to bully people into buying you things?"

"It depends."

I crossed my arms over my puffy purple coat. "So you aren't going to do anything?"

"I'll check up on them. I was planning on it anyway. Don't call Sheriff Malone about this. He's busy."

"Yes, I know. That's why I came to you."

"I don't want you snooping around those kids, either. Leave it to me. I know that's not your strong suit."

I ground my teeth together and nodded. There was nothing else to say, so I left. Light snow was falling, but we hadn't had a bad storm in a few weeks. This was my first winter in Kansas, and I was ready for it to end.

The library wasn't in my plans, but I stopped anyway. It had been a while since I'd gotten a book. The library appeared empty. Brian wasn't even at his desk. I walked around for a minute until I found him in the children's section. He stood on a step stool, rearranging a tall bulletin board on the wall. A bunch of construction paper shapes littered the floor beneath him.

"Hi, Brian," I said.

He turned and grinned. "Ivy! It's been a while."

"Yeah, I haven't had time to read."

He stepped down and ran a hand over his curly black hair. "I heard about the Clementses. You didn't even come to me for help solving the murder. I'm feeling a bit left out." He smiled and tacked something to the board.

I nodded. "We were snowed in at the Clementses'. And that happened when the cell tower was down. We couldn't ask anyone for help."

"Well, that makes me feel better." He laughed. Brian was an easygoing guy. I should be more like him.

"What are you up to?" I asked.

"I like to change the boards for each season. I figure if I decorate for spring, this horrible winter might go away."

I laughed. "Good luck with that."

"It would be finished already, but I had this group of kids come through, and I thought they would never leave. I had to watch them because they kept messing with things."

"Little kids?"

"No, they weren't really kids. Livy was with them, so probably her age."

"They came to the diner yesterday."

"They're an odd bunch. None of them would get a library card. They made Livy check out everything they wanted."

"I'm nervous about them," I admitted. "I think someone's taking advantage of having followers."

"I think you're right. There was one boy they called Joseph or Jacob. He seemed to be telling everyone what to do."

"I noticed that. Ledford knows about them, but I don't think he'll do anything. I'm not sure there's anything he can do."

"Groups like that always get into trouble, eventually."

"Don't you ever get bored here?" I asked. "I hardly ever see anyone in here."

"I'm easily entertained. I have all the books I could ever read. When I feel like I've been too lazy, I do squats in my office."

"Any book suggestions? I'm dying to read a good mystery."

"Hmm. There are a few new books on my desk. I haven't had time to look at them, but you're welcome to take one. I think I saw one written by one of the ghostwriters who did some of the *Nancy Drew* books."

"Ghostwriters? Carolyn Keene wrote *Nancy Drew*."

Brian pursed his lips together and patted my shoulder. "I hate to be the one to ruin your day, but Carolyn Keene doesn't exist."

I frowned. "What do you mean?"

"A publishing house made outlines and hired people to write them. There were quite a few who worked on them over the years."

"No!" I said, crossing my arms. "How could I not know that?"

"It's not something they advertise. It was the same with *The Hardy Boys*."

"Thanks a lot, Brian. That's going to ruin my day, and possibly my week," I teased.

"Hey, you don't want to live in ignorance, do you?"

"Maybe. There's happiness in ignorance."

My phone buzzed, and I pulled it out. "José needs me at the diner. I'll come back later for a book."

"Hang on." He pulled his wallet from his pocket and handed me a few bills. "When you come back, will you bring me a few cookies? Since the library and diner have similar hours, I never seem to get over there."

"Sure. You can call anytime, and I'd be happy to bring you something."

"Thanks."

I made my way back to the diner, and when I got inside, it was chaos. Livy's friends were back, acting like a bunch of unruly teens. I wondered if they had all been expelled and just said they had dropped out. It wouldn't surprise me. Two girls were leaping across the floor and spinning. One group tossed crumpled-up napkins back and forth, and one boy stood on a stool cheering. There weren't any other customers. They'd probably been scared away.

"Stop!" I yelled. Livy sat in one booth with her head on the table. A few of them stopped but then went back to what they were doing.

José came over to me. "I tried kicking them out, but they won't listen. There are too many of them."

"Stop, or you are all banned from the diner!" I shouted.

Jacob sat at the table across from Livy. "Don't be so uptight," he said. "You should be happy we're enjoying your place."

I looked at the mess all over the floor. "You're making a mess! Get out."

Jacob's eyes pierced mine. "We aren't ready."

My eyes narrowed, and I pulled out my phone. I didn't know who I would call, but it made most of them nervous, and they rushed out the door.

"Livy, can I see you in the kitchen?" I asked.

Livy sat up and slowly came toward me.

Jacob grabbed her arm and pulled her back. "She doesn't work for you anymore."

Livy looked from where he held her arm to me. I wanted to grab her other arm, but that would only start a tug-of-war, and Livy didn't look up to it.

"That doesn't mean I can't talk to her," I said.

"I said she isn't talking to you," he said.

José tossed his hairnet to the side and stomped over to Jacob. "You have three seconds to let her go."

Jacob smiled. "Or what, old man?"

"One, two, three," José said quickly. He pulled back his fist and punched Jacob in the face. He fell to the floor and released Livy. Livy let out a sob and ran to the kitchen.

"You probably broke my cheek!" Jacob said from the floor.

"And I'll break the other one if you don't get out of here! One—"

Jacob was up and running from the diner. José didn't mess around when he counted.

I turned to José. "I didn't know you had that in you."

He grinned. "We all have a past. Go check on Livy, and I'll clean this up."

I went into the kitchen to find Livy sobbing on Anton's shoulder. Anton's eyes were wide, and he was stiff. He looked like he was trying to decide whether to run or pat her back.

"Livy?" I said. She turned and released Anton.

She sniffed. "I'm sorry."

"We need to get those people out of Muddy Creek," I said.

She swallowed. "I can't. I promised they could stay."

"Do you really enjoy living in a snow cave?"

"No, but I have to."

"You don't."

She rubbed her eyes. "It would have been fine if Jacob hadn't joined. We were all doing great without him. We put Noah in charge, but then Jacob came and started bossing everyone around."

"I don't think you should go back," I said. "I have an extra room now. You can stay with me."

She shook her head. "I have to go back. I made a commitment."

"Things change. What does Carlos think about all of it?"

She frowned. "I don't know. We don't talk a lot."

"Oh. I thought you were dating."

Livy wrinkled her nose. "I would never date any of those guys."

"He had his arm around you, so I just assumed."

She rolled her eyes. "Everyone in that group is really huggy. It's annoying. It's hard to walk anywhere without one of them putting their arm over me."

"I think you should stay with Ivy," Anton said.

Livy looked up at him and tilted her head. "You do?"

"Yeah. Those people don't seem stable."

She shook her head. "Maybe later, but right now, I can't. I need to go." She turned and hurried away.

I sighed.

"Can't you make her stay?" Anton asked. His brown eyes flashed with something I'd never seen in them. Maybe Carrie had been right. Maybe Anton did like Livy.

"I can't tie her down. She's her own person."

He nodded. "I bet you could find something illegal about those guys. Then she would have to leave them."

"I thought you were against snooping?"

He shrugged. "I usually am. You do some pretty crazy things. This is different, though. Livy's our friend. Those other people you put yourself in danger for were practically strangers."

Anton hated the fact that we had solved some murders. He'd managed to stay out of a lot of them, but he'd been right in the middle of the last one, and he'd been terrified.

José came into the kitchen with an armful of garbage. He dumped it into the bin. "I think they stole some of the silverware and some other things."

I groaned. "Like what?"

"Saltshakers and a syrup dispenser."

"Do I ban them?"

José shrugged. "I would. Especially that Jacob. He's a bossy one. I'm surprised all those kids listen to him. He screamed at one of them for ordering fish because he was allergic. They weren't even sitting near him."

"I talked to Ledford. I can't tell if he'll do anything. Did they scare away customers?"

"No. There's not usually a lot of people on Tuesday mornings."

The back door opened, and Boyd came in holding Creepers's leash. "It's cold out there. Creepers and I went for a walk. I let him back into your place." I couldn't believe Creepers let Boyd take him for walks. If I tried to leash him, he hissed and bit at me.

"I saw all those corn kids running down the road laughing," Boyd said.

I grinned. "Corn kids?"

"That's what I'm calling them."

"I need to make cookies. I told Brian I'd take him some."

"I could use a cookie," Boyd said, sitting at the island while I got the mixer ready.

I rubbed my lips together. "Do we have any servers here?"

José shook his head. "The corn kids made Sarah cry, so I let her go home. I only schedule one server for Tuesday morning and afternoon."

"I can help," Anton offered. "There isn't a lot to cook today, anyway."

"I need a new cookie recipe," I said. "I'm getting sick of this one."

Boyd's mouth turned down. "If it's not broken, don't fix it."

José laughed. "That's Boyd's way of saying he isn't sick of your cookies."

"I saw Jett drive into town," Boyd said.

I looked up. "Are you sure?"

He grinned. "Of course I'm sure. Who else drives a Cybertruck with police lights? That was the best investment I ever made. I made him promise to take me places whenever I want.”

Boyd had gotten Jett a Cybertruck after his truck had blown up. He said it was a nice tax write-off.

“You probably shouldn’t have said anything,” José said. “Ivy’s cheeks look nice and smooth, and you know what happens when she’s around Jett.”

Anton’s eyes narrowed. “What happens?”

I felt my face burn red, and I threw a rag at José.

Boyd slapped his leg and laughed. “That scruff on Jett’s face really does a number on Ivy’s.”

Anton blinked, then smiled. “Oh, I get it.”

“You guys are ridiculous. You know who pays you, right?” I asked, grabbing some butter from the fridge.

“You don’t pay me,” Boyd said.

“But I give you cookies.”

“That’s true.”

“I’m surprised Ivy hasn’t run off to mess up her face,” José said. “We won’t stop you. You know we can make the cookies, right?”

I frowned and unwrapped the butter. “I’m not going.” If I thought Jett wanted to see me, I might.

“I’m sure he’ll be around,” Boyd said.

I put the butter in the bowl and tried to think of something else. I had a lot to think about, and having the stress of wondering what Jett was thinking would have to wait.

Chapter 4

If Brian wasn't such a good friend, I wouldn't have gone back with the cookies. The air was frigid, and I was tired. I walked through the snow with a tray. It had a covered plate of José's enchiladas and a smaller plate of cookies.

I walked into the library and put it on Brian's desk. Voices came from the nonfiction section, so I followed them. Brian and Jett stood talking. My heart stopped. It felt like forever since I'd seen Jett. His eyes looked tired. He smiled at me but didn't come near.

"Hey, Ivy," Brian said.

"Hi. I brought your cookies. I brought some of José's enchiladas, too. They're on your desk."

His eyes lit up. "Thanks! You didn't have to do that."

"We had too many. It's been a slow day."

I looked at Jett. He wasn't exactly glaring at Brian, but it was close. "How long are you here?" I asked him.

He looked at me, and his expression didn't improve. "Just for the night. I have to be back in Wichita in the morning."

There was no point in telling him about Livy. He wouldn't have time to do anything, anyway.

Jett's serious stare made me fidget.

"I have to go," I said. "I'll see you guys later." I hurried out of the library without a book again. Why had things gotten weird with Jett? They'd always been strange, but this was different. He'd looked happy to see me but then looked annoyed.

I dashed down the street, ignoring the bitter wind.

"Miss Clark!" Jett called. I stopped and waited for him to jog up to me. "Are there any more cookies at the diner?"

I smiled but felt funny. He'd called me Miss Clark. "Of course." We walked quietly, and I was all too aware he wasn't holding my hand.

"Do you take Brian dinner a lot?" he asked.

"No. That was the only time."

"Hmm."

Something stirred in me. He'd teased me about Brian before. That was why he'd acted the way he had. He was jealous. That had to be a good sign, didn't it? But what was up with calling me Miss Clark?

"Brian ordered some cookies, and I thought I might as well bring him some food. It would be sad to let that good food go to waste. You're welcome to have some. I should take some to Ledford. It might make him hate me less."

"It's possible. I think he might be mellowing a bit."

We went into the diner, and he followed me into the kitchen.

José turned. "Hey, Jett. Do you want an enchilada?"

"Sure," he said, sitting at the island. "I've been eating fast food all week, and I feel like garbage."

I raised my eyebrow. "Didn't you just say you wanted a cookie?"

He grinned. "I just wanted a reason to walk with you."

Anton turned from where he was washing a pot. "It looks like all they did was walk. Ivy doesn't have any whisker burns."

"Anton!" I said, putting my hands on my hips. "If you start acting like Boyd and José, I'll put you on permanent toilet-cleaning duty!"

José laughed and put a plate in front of Jett. "He only said what we were all thinking."

Jett smiled and cut his enchilada. "Come on, guys. I'm on duty. I can't be on vacation all the time."

An immense weight lifted from me. Every time Jett had kissed me, he had been technically on vacation. He'd been working every time I'd seen him since. He still could send better texts, though.

The bell to the diner rang, and Livy and four of her friends entered.

"I guess punching Jacob in the face didn't scare him away," I said. He had a huge bruise on his cheek. Trina led them to a booth and began talking to them.

"Perhaps not," José said, "but I bet they behave this time."

"What happened?" Jett asked. José gave him a quick update.

Trina came in. "Five stacks of pancakes."

José frowned. "Pancakes? Not enchiladas?"

Trina smiled. "I tried."

The group was better behaved today. Maybe because there were only the five of them, or they were scared of José. They weren't even talking loud. Today, Noah sat by Livy, and Hannah glared at them.

I grabbed a rag and washed off the island. It wasn't dirty, but I felt like I needed to keep busy.

"Someone do something!" Hannah suddenly yelled.

José stood, but Jett shook his head. "I've got it." He went into the dining area. I didn't even want to know what they were doing. Grabbing the garbage, I took it outside. I breathed in the crisp air and stood staring out at the snow. Kansas seemed to go on forever, and the diner was on the edge of the town square. That made the view incredible during sunsets.

I went back in and glanced around. José was gone, and Anton was on his phone giving the address of the diner. Lots of people were talking in the dining area, and it sounded like they were panicking. I frowned and walked toward the door. Anton grabbed my arm and shook his head.

"Thank you," he said, and he hung up. "I guess I don't have to stop you. You've seen dead people before."

My heart sped up. "Dead people?"

"Jacob just had an allergic reaction. He's dead."

"That fast?"

"I guess."

I walked out and joined the small crowd. Jacob's body was on the floor.

Hannah was crying. "He used his EpiPen, and it didn't work."

Jett looked up. "Anton, call Ledford."

"Alright," Anton said from the other room.

Livy stood against the wall, hugging herself, and Hannah sobbed from her seat. Noah tried to look upset, but his eyes gave him away. Carlos leaned over the table and looked curious but not upset.

"Nobody touches anything," Jett said. "I want you all to get away from the table."

"Why?" Noah asked. "He had an allergic reaction. There's nothing suspicious about that."

Jett's eyes locked on Noah's. "I said, get away from the table."

Noah's eyes narrowed, but he did as he was told. Noah, Hannah, and Carlos all joined Livy by the wall.

Jett stood and scanned the table. I didn't look at the body. If Jett said he was dead, that was good enough for me.

The door flew open, and Ledford ran in. He glared as he looked around the room. "There are too many people in here," he said, walking up to Livy and the other three. He stood at his full height, which was about as tall as me, and puffed out his chest. "I want the four of you to go sit in that booth on the other side of the room."

He glanced at me and José. "Do you have to be here?"

Jett rolled his eyes. "They work here."

Ledford nodded and pulled gloves over his hands. He began examining items on the table.

"It was an allergy," Noah called. "He's super allergic to fish."

Ledford glared over at him. "I don't see any fish here."

"I have to leave early tomorrow. I'll leave this to you," Jett said, looking at Ledford.

Ledford peered at me. "Did you hear that? Me, not Ivy Clark."

"Calm down, Ledford," Jett said.

I shrugged. I solved mysteries, not accidental deaths. The entire thing was sad, but not what I looked into. I was worried about what this might do to the diner. It wasn't good to have someone die when they were eating at your business.

Ledford unscrewed the lid to the syrup. He smelled it and frowned. "You have fish-flavored syrup?"

"What? No," I said. "Only maple syrup."

"Smell this." He stuck it under my nose, and I sniffed. I wrinkled my nose. It smelled fishy. He held it up to Jett, and he smelled it.

I pointed at the table. "There are two bottles of syrup on the table. We only ever put one."

José gestured at the four friends. "Last time they were here, they stole silverware and a syrup dispenser."

Ledford looked at me. "This is a crime scene. Close the diner."

I nodded, went to the window, and flipped the sign to Closed. There wasn't anyone here, anyway. This was just great. My diner was a crime scene, and I would have to deal with Ledford.

Jett pulled a freezer bag from his pocket and held it open. Ledford placed the syrup dispenser inside, and Jett carefully closed it. He pulled out another bag, and Ledford picked up the EpiPen from the floor and placed it in the bag.

I went into the kitchen. I would normally try to figure out what had happened, but if Jett wasn't leading the investigation, I would only annoy Ledford, and nothing would get done.

Anton was sitting on a stool eating an enchilada. "I swear, this stuff follows you guys."

"It seems that way." I sat on another stool and yawned.

"At least it wasn't a murder this time. I've had enough of that."

I cringed. "It looks like someone might have tampered with the syrup."

He sighed. "I would quit, but I've seen all the murder mysteries."

I cocked my head. "What do you mean?"

He smiled. "Everywhere the sleuth goes, people get killed, but they're usually people who aren't main characters. I'm considering myself a main character in your life, so I should be safe."

"I'll stay out of this one. Jett put Ledford in charge."

"I don't blame you. I wouldn't work with that guy."

"You can go home. We had to close."

He nodded. "How's Livy?"

"I'm not sure. She's out there. I'm going to ask her to stay with me again. I don't like the thought of her sleeping in a snow cave, especially when someone in her group might be a murderer."

"Good idea."

"Alright, listen," Ledford boomed out. "The four of you are not to leave town. Do you understand? You can stay at the B&B or go back to your snow caves, but don't leave, or I will assume you are guilty."

I peeked out the window. "Livy can stay with me," I said.

Livy gave a small smile.

Ledford rubbed his mustache. "First, I want all of you in the sheriff's office. I need to talk to all of you."

"Do you want help?" Jett asked.

"Nope. I'm going to have this all solved by the time you come back from your trials at the end of the week."

Hannah wiped at her eyes. "Why would anyone kill Jacob? I don't understand."

Noah looked at her. "Are you serious? The guy was the biggest jerk I've ever met. I bet everyone in camp wanted to kill him."

"I'll have to go talk to all of them as well," Ledford said. "They could have been involved."

"I'm going to the B&B," Carlos said. "I'm tired of sleeping in the snow. That was only fun the first few days. I'd rather be going to school."

Chapter 5

I sat on my recliner, and Livy sat on the sofa. Creepers had taken a liking to her and sat on her lap. We both held mugs of hot chocolate.

"Did you call your parents?" I asked.

"Yes. I thought they should know the police would be around the property. My dad is mad. He didn't want me to quit school, and now this."

"I would imagine. Why did you quit?"

She sighed. "It's complicated. I didn't actually want to go to college. I want to be a cosmetologist. My parents wanted me to go to an actual college. I was about to tell them I wanted to go to cosmetology school, but then I met a guy."

I sipped my hot chocolate. "Oh?"

She placed her mug on a coaster on the coffee table. "Yeah, it's stupid. I wanted to stick to my cosmetology plan, but it cost more than the college my parents wanted me to attend. I stuck to the plan and hoped the guy might wake up and notice me if I was leaving and ask me to stay."

"And he didn't?"

She raked a hand through her long red hair. "No. We were only ever friends and not even close friends, so it was stupid of me to think it would change anything. So I went to college, and I hated it. I met Noah, and he had this plan. He held meetings and told us about what a waste of time college was. He said we could live off the land and blah, blah, blah. It sounded stupid, but also like a nice escape. I told them we could stay on my parents' farm for a while."

"How does Jacob fit in?"

"He started coming to the meetings. When Noah would talk, Jacob would interrupt. He eventually took over, and everyone forgot that it was Noah's idea because Jacob had a big personality. Noah was really mad. No one liked Jacob, but for some reason, we all followed him."

"He had a lot of enemies?"

"Tons. He said we all needed to share everything and take care of each other, but I never saw him share anything. He was just taking advantage of the rest of us being stupid." She grabbed her mug and took a swallow.

"Do you have any idea who might have done it?"

"No. If I were to take a guess, I would say Noah. Jacob ruined his dream and took it over. He also spent a lot of time trying to hit on Hannah."

"Are Hannah and Noah a couple?" I asked.

"Off and on. Hannah has a temper, and Noah doesn't like that. Yet they always somehow end up back together."

"Are you good friends with them?"

"I've only known them since the second week of January. We get along fine, but I wouldn't say we're close."

"What about Carlos?"

"He just seems along for the ride. He was failing all his classes and figured he might as well leave. I like him more than the others."

I took a sip from my mug. "What happened with the guy you liked before?"

She rolled her eyes. "He's still here, not into me."

"Anton?"

She blushed and ducked her head. "Yes."

"Isn't he a little old for you?"

"I'm almost twenty, and he's twenty-five. Five years isn't a lot. It doesn't matter since he doesn't care."

"I doubt he knows."

"I've been obvious."

"Do you know Anton? You might have to say it to his face, then stop and let him process it, then say it again."

"No way. If he rejects me outright, I can't take that. Has he been dating while I've been gone?"

"He went on one date that I know of with a girl he met online. That was a month ago, and I've never heard about a follow-up date."

"We used to sit outside in the back of the diner and talk during our breaks. He's a good guy."

"He is."

Livy yawned. "Is it alright if I go to bed?"

"Yep. Let me show you the room."

I led her to my spare room and went back for Creepers. This was such a mess. I hoped it would clear up quickly and Ledford would have answers soon. He didn't want us to go into the diner until he said it was clear. He'd put crime scene tape all over the place, causing everyone who walked by to stop and stare. This wasn't good for business.

❧

I woke up the following morning to someone beating on my door. Grabbing my robe, I hurried to the door. Having a door going from outside to my apartment was nice. I didn't have to walk down to the diner to talk to people. Deputy Ledford stood there holding a pair of handcuffs. My mouth turned down. This couldn't be good.

"May I speak to Livy?"

Livy walked into view. She was already dressed for the day. She looked at the handcuffs and frowned.

Ledford pushed past me. "Your fingerprints were found on the EpiPen that Jacob McComb used last night."

Livy swallowed and nodded. "He dropped it in the snow yesterday. I picked it up and handed it to him."

Ledford's eyebrow raised. "The EpiPen had been replaced by a fake. It had poison in it, so not only did it not work, it killed him faster. The only fingerprints were yours and his."

Her eyes went wide, and I frowned. I only knew Livy from working with her, but I found it hard to believe she was a killer. She was reliable and always jumped in to help.

"I didn't do it," Livy insisted.

"What about the syrup dispenser?" I asked.

"It had everyone's fingerprints except Hannah Taylor's."

"She doesn't eat a lot of sugar," Livy muttered.

"The only evidence you have is fingerprints on one thing. She told you she touched it. I don't think you can take her in for that."

Ledford glared at me and held up the handcuffs. Livy held out her wrists. He cuffed her and began spouting off her rights. Creepers looked curiously at everyone but decided it wasn't worth his time and wandered away.

"Miss Clark?" Ledford said, pulling my attention back to him. "I saw your cat in the diner yesterday. That's a health code violation. Don't let me see him down there again."

I nodded. I'd been trying to keep him in my apartment since it was bigger now, but he slipped out occasionally. Boyd now had a key to my apartment so he could play with Creepers during the day. It helped both of them stay busy.

"Ivy?" Livy said, her eyes pleading with mine. "You'll prove I'm innocent, right?"

Ledford growled. He actually growled. "That is not Miss Clark's job. If you are innocent, I will be the one to prove it. For now, there is enough evidence to take you in. Do you understand?"

Livy's lip trembled, but she nodded. As they were leaving, Livy looked over her shoulder, and I gave her a thumbs-up. It wouldn't be easy to work with Ledford as the lead in the case, but I would do my best. Livy smiled slightly.

I slipped on my snow boots and followed them down the wooden stairs and into the area behind the diner.

Anton was about to go in the back kitchen door, and he frowned. "Why is she cuffed?"

"Because she killed Jacob McComb," Ledford said.

Anton frowned and crossed his arms. "No way. Livy would never hurt anyone."

"There's plenty of evidence."

"That could have been planted," I said.

"How would someone plant her fingerprints?" Ledford asked.

The back door opened, and José peeked out. I really had slept in. He looked from Livy to Anton and frowned.

"Let her go," Anton said. "You've got the wrong person." He made a fist and took a step toward Ledford. Anton was probably a little under six feet, but he looked big standing by Ledford. A fight still might go badly for him because Ledford was in good shape.

"Go into the diner and mind your own business," Ledford said.

"Livy's my friend. It is my business."

Ledford smiled. "I think you should choose your friends more carefully."

Anton sprang forward, but José was ready. He grabbed Anton by the arm and held him back.

Ledford laughed and pulled on Livy's arm as he began walking away.

Anton yanked against José's grip, but José wasn't letting go. "So what? You're going to make her walk across town like that? Where's your car?"

Ledford kept walking. "It's too close to drive a car." He turned and looked pointedly at me. "Miss Clark? We don't need to bother Sheriff Malone with this. He has two trials going on, and he's stressed. He can't do anything here. Telling him about it will only add to the stress."

I nodded. I hated to agree with Ledford, but I knew he was right.

Anton was still struggling against José. José pushed him into the diner, and I followed them and shut the door.

"Let go!" Anton said.

"So you can what?" José asked, releasing him. "You're no good to her if you're locked up too, and Ledford could take you easily."

Anton took a deep breath and looked at me. "What are we going to do?"

I bit my lip.

"First, Ivy should probably go get dressed," José suggested.

I looked down at my pink robe and sighed. It was good the diner didn't open for fifteen more minutes.

"Second, someone should take Livy her coat. Ledford didn't have the decency to let her grab it before they left."

"I'll take it," Anton said.

José shook his head. "That would be a bad idea."

The back door opened, and Carrie came in. Her eyes scanned everyone, and she frowned when she stopped on me.

"I know, I'm getting dressed." I left the kitchen and ran up to my room. The door was locked. I sighed. I didn't want to go outside in my robe again, but Jett had put quality locks on my doors. Busting in would take too long and ruin the door. I hurried back past everyone in the kitchen, then went out the door and up the stairs.

I pulled the door open, and Creepers met me. He was probably waiting for breakfast. I went into the kitchen and grabbed a can of cat food from the pantry. I popped the top and put it on the floor. I usually put it in a bowl, but I was in a hurry.

After I was ready for the day, I went back to the diner kitchen. José was frying bacon, and Carrie was scrambling eggs. Anton had his hairnet on, but he was pacing back and forth. When he saw me, he stopped.

"Let's go solve this murder," he said.

I arched my brow. "I thought you weren't into solving murders?"

"I am now."

"Do you need us?" I asked.

José shook his head. "Nope. Go."

I grabbed my purple coat from a hook by the door, and Anton grabbed his jacket. I had no idea what we were going to do, but doing nothing wasn't going to work for Anton. We walked around the diner to my car and climbed in.

Boyd came riding up on his electric bike. I couldn't figure out how he wasn't slipping on the ice. He jumped off and waved, so I rolled down the window. "Where are you going? I just heard about Livy."

I frowned. "From who?"

"Barbra."

"How did she know? Never mind, just get in."

Boyd leaned his bike against the building and hopped in the back. "What's the plan?" he asked as he buckled his seat belt.

"We don't have a plan," I said.

"Let's go to the commune and see what's going on there," Anton said.

"It's not a commune," I explained. "Just a bunch of college kids."

"It's a commune," Anton pointed out. "I heard them saying they share everything, and they're all being bossed around by their leader."

"I'm calling them the corn kids," Boyd said. "It makes it easy."

Chapter 6

I pulled my gray Kia Soul from the parking space, and Boyd gave me directions to the Smith's farm. When we were near, we drove around for a few minutes before we found the camp. I stopped the car and scanned the area. I couldn't believe anyone was living here. There were several things that looked like poorly constructed igloos and one large heavy-duty tent. In the middle of the snow caves, a fire was burning.

People sat on logs around the flames. They all looked tired and miserable. I wondered if they had been like this before the murder.

"Let's go," Anton said, jumping out of the car.

"He's never been one to volunteer for these things," Boyd said, rubbing his goatee.

"That's because no one's ever accused Livy of murder before."

"Ah. That's how it is. I've wondered about the two of them."

I got out and slammed the door.

We walked toward the fire, and Noah came toward us. He had on an overstuffed coat and a thick winter hat.

"Welcome," he said. "How can we help you?"

"Tell us who killed Jacob," Anton demanded, clenching his fists. I frowned. I hoped Anton would make it through the day without hitting anyone.

Noah frowned. "I wish we knew."

"I know it wasn't Livy."

"Of course it wasn't. No one said it was."

"She's been arrested," I said.

Hannah left her seat by the fire. Two blond braids hung to her shoulders, and she wore a black beanie. "Why would anyone arrest Livy?"

"That's not why we're here," Anton said. "We're here to find the real killer."

Hannah rubbed her eyes. "As soon as this is over, I'm leaving. I'm tired of all this."

"You can't leave," Noah said. "You need to help us build a new life."

Hannah rolled her eyes. "Whatever." She went and sat back down.

"Do you want breakfast?" Noah asked.

"No, thank you," I said.

Noah walked to the fire and grabbed a basket that was sitting nearby. He walked to us and held it out. "Are you sure?"

I looked inside, and my forehead furrowed. "What is that? It looks like weeds."

"Dead weeds," Boyd said.

Noah grinned. "We only eat things that grow in our area. It's good for your body to only eat natural plants."

Hannah groaned and covered her face.

"You definitely ate more than dead weeds at the diner," Anton said.

Noah nodded. "We had some moments of weakness caused by Jacob. Now that he is no longer with us, we will go back to the way things should have been." Noah clapped and called out, "We have guests! It's time for entertainment."

"We aren't here for entertainment," I said.

Boyd grinned. "I wouldn't mind. I bet it makes a good story."

Noah clapped. "Come on, Dean."

A boy at the fire picked up a guitar and started playing. Two girls who were wrapped in blankets stood and dropped their blankets. They were wearing long white dresses and had fake flowers in their braids. They picked up baskets and began leaping across the trampled snow. Reaching into their baskets, they tossed fake flower petals as they danced. The others in the group began singing, except Hannah, who looked like she wanted to cry or possibly hit someone.

"What the trash," Anton muttered under his breath.

Boyd began clapping, which added to the ridiculousness of it all. The song wasn't meant to be clapped to. A woman came over and handed Ivy an ugly fake flower, then she turned and put one behind Boyd's ear.

When she walked up to Anton, he held up his hand. "Don't touch me." She frowned and walked back to her log. When the song ended, Boyd and Noah clapped. Boyd walked over to a log and stepped up on it.

"Gather around," Boyd said. Anton and I shared a concerned look. Boyd might do anything. A group of about ten came. "Is this everyone?"

"Livy and Carlos are in town, and three are out foraging for food," Noah said.

Boyd nodded. "I have something to say. You all are the biggest bunch of idiots I've ever seen."

"Boyd," I warned.

He ignored me. "You can't live off weeds in the cold, singing and dancing like fools. You're all going to end up dead. Is that what you want?"

"We're thriving," Noah said. "We have plenty. Plenty of corn got left behind after the harvest."

Hannah began sobbing. We might have to take her with us.

"Who are you? The mayor or something?" someone asked.

"No," Boyd said. "I'm just a guy who isn't stupid, and I have a lot to say." He gave me a look, and I frowned. Did he really think I could go snooping while he talked? There was no way he could keep this group's attention for long. "Where's Livy's cave? My friend Ivy's going to look inside."

"It's that one." Noah pointed. "Now, what do you have to say?"

Boyd began telling a story, and I went into Livy's cave. It was warmer than being outside because there was no wind. The cave was almost tall enough for me to stand, but I had to slouch. There was a sleeping bag and a small bag on the floor. I pulled some gloves from my purse and put them on.

I looked through Livy's bag but found nothing unusual. Ledford had probably been through everything already. I moved the sleeping bag and didn't see anything. I left the igloo and saw all the people hanging on Boyd's every word.

"And that was the second time I was mistaken for Dwayne 'The Rock' Johnson," Boyd said.

I shook my head and slipped into the next cave. Nothing interesting in there. I pushed some things around and looked under the sleeping bag. These people really only had the essentials. I left the cave and looked around.

"It was rough," Boyd said, "but we left the gold behind." My eyes narrowed. Anton folded his arms against the cold and grinned as he listened to Boyd.

I went into the next igloo, and it was empty. I wondered if it was Jacob's. The hard-packed snow gave me pause. All the igloos had packed floors, but if I was going to hide anything, I would hide it under the snow. I used my boot to push the snow around, but I found nothing.

The icy wind blasted my face when I came out. I wondered if I could get into the tent without being noticed.

"The bear wasn't even fazed," Boyd continued. "Can you imagine what would have happened if we hadn't known the bologna trick?"

Getting into the tent was a breeze. Whatever Boyd was saying was keeping them all distracted. The tent must be for supplies. Several boxes were stacked around the sides. I opened one and saw cans of pears. Why were they eating old corn if they had food? I moved the box and opened the one beneath it. More fruit.

I moved boxes until I got to the bottom box. I opened it and frowned. It was filled to the top with small ziplock bags full of white powder. There was no way Ledford would have missed this. I grabbed one and shoved it in my purse. I returned everything to the way it was and put my gloves back in my purse.

The tent flap opened, and Noah came in. He smiled. "Hey, what are you doing in here?"

I tried to look normal. "Just looking. You seem to have a lot of food. Why aren't you eating it?"

"We eat that once weekly just to get something different."

I nodded. "Good idea."

"We need it to last."

"So all the boxes are full of food?"

"Yes."

"Maybe you should give some to Hannah. She looks like she might need something."

Noah shook his head. "Hannah's just dramatic. We both grew up with money, so it's hard for her to walk away from that." I remembered Jacob making Noah pay. That meant they still had some money. Noah had looked like the poor picked-on guy at the diner, and now he was the crazy leader.

We left the tent. I couldn't go in any more caves because Noah would see. I waved at Boyd so he would stop talking.

He nodded at me. "So the moral of the story is if you want to keep your hair, stay away from Minnesota, at least the northeast area. That's all I have for you today."

The people around the fire clapped, and Boyd stepped down from the log. We said goodbye and got into the car.

"Those people were sure hanging on your words," I observed.

Boyd laughed. "They're desperate for entertainment, is all."

"Dwayne Johnson?" Anton said. "You weren't even trying to sound realistic."

"Are you saying I don't look like The Rock?" Boyd
asked, leaning forward.

Anton grinned. "I'd say you are closer to Danny DeVi-
to."

Boyd roared with laughter. "Let's say I'm somewhere in
the middle."

"Did you find anything?" Anton asked.

"I found a box full of sandwich bags of white powder."

"Interesting," Anton said. "Do we tell Ledford?"

I chewed my lip. "We might have to. He's going to be
mad we came. I put a bag in my purse."

Anton smacked his head. "Why?"

"Just in case they move it or something."

"What if we get pulled over and we have drugs?"

I tilted my head and looked at him as I began driving.
"Who's going to pull us over? Jett's out of town, and
Ledford's busy. And we don't know it's drugs. It could be
flour or something. I didn't have time to check."

"Who puts flour into baggies?" Anton asked.

I shrugged. "I'm not saying it's not drugs. I'm just saying
we don't know."

"If you take it to Ledford, Livy might be in more trouble."

"I bet most of the people there don't even know about
it."

"Do you think they'll notice you took one?"

"I doubt it. There were a bunch of bags, so they would have to count them to know. My question is, who knows about the drugs if they are drugs? Was it Jacob or Noah? My guess is one of them. If it was Jacob, Noah might not know anything about it."

"Are you taking the bag to Ledford? He might arrest you," Anton said.

"For what?" Boyd asked. "Drugs or for talking to the corn kids?"

"Either."

"I doubt Ledford would arrest me, although I'm thinking I shouldn't have taken the baggie. If I hadn't, I wouldn't have to tell Ledford anything."

Boyd pulled out his phone. "I'm calling Jett."

"No!" I protested. "Ledford was right. Jett has a lot on his mind. Let's not make it worse."

"The more you hide, the worse it gets." Boyd pushed something on his phone, and I pursed my lips. He put the phone on speakerphone, and I hoped Jett wouldn't answer.

"Hello?" Jett said.

"Hey, Jett. Boyd here. Also, Ivy and Anton. Do you have a minute?"

"I have five minutes before I have to go testify."

"We have a hypothetical question."

"Shoot."

"Say we went to a commune outside town and found a box full of what might be drugs. What if Ivy took some and put them in her purse for evidence?"

"That would be a bad idea." Jett sighed.

"Just suppose that's what happened. What would the best thing be to do next? Tell Deputy Ledford? Throw them away and pretend it didn't happen? Dump them on Mayor Jepson since he's probably crooked anyway?"

I took a deep breath through my nose and let it out slowly.

"Ivy?" Jett said. "Do you have drugs in your purse?"

I cleared my throat. "Didn't you hear Boyd? It's hypothetical."

His sigh was loud enough to hear over the phone. "I would say to take them to Ledford and beg for mercy."

"That doesn't sound pleasant," Anton said.

"Anton? How did you get mixed up in this?" Jett asked. "You usually avoid these things."

"Hypothetical, remember?" I said. "We're gonna let you go now. Good luck with everything."

"We didn't tell him about Livy," Anton said.

"What's wrong with Livy?" he asked.

"Nothing to worry about. Bye. Hang up, Boyd."

Boyd hung up, and I sighed. "Jett needs a clear mind. Now he's going to be worried about whatever we're doing."

"What are we doing?" Boyd asked.

"I'll drop you two at the diner. Then I'm going to talk to Ledford."

"Alone?" Anton asked.

"Yep. I don't trust you to act rationally regarding Livy, and Boyd might say something to make it worse."

"What do you mean?" Anton asked. "I'm rational about Livy. Ledford's a moron."

"That's why you aren't coming."

Chapter 7

After I dropped them off, I got out and walked to the sheriff's office. I took a stabilizing breath before entering.

A middle-aged woman with dark brown hair and round glasses sat at the front desk. I remembered hearing something about Jett hiring a secretary. She smiled at me, and I looked behind her to Ledford. He sat at a desk behind her, typing on his computer. He looked up when I entered, and his face fell. I felt a little bad because of his reaction to me.

"What?" he asked.

I swallowed. "Umm... so... well... I..."

"Just say it," Ledford said. "I'm sure it won't make me think worse of you. What have you been doing that you shouldn't?"

I sat in the chair across from him. This wasn't easy. I wondered what the secretary was thinking. "I went to the cornfield."

"What a surprise," he said sarcastically. "I already searched it."

"Did you search the tent?"

"Yes. It's just canned food."

I grabbed my purse and dumped it on the table. "And this." The bag fell out along with my wallet and phone. I grabbed my stuff and put it back.

His eyes narrowed, and he grabbed a pair of plastic gloves from his desk. He took the bag and opened it, then smelled it. "Cocaine. Where was it?"

"There's a big box at the bottom of all the other boxes. It's full of bags like that."

He scratched his head and glared at me. I fidgeted. It wasn't my fault his search hadn't been thorough.

"Can I talk to Livy?" I asked.

"No."

"Why?"

"I need to talk to her. You need to mind your own business."

I opened my mouth to speak but shut it when he glared. "You could get in a lot of trouble for this," he said, pointing at the baggie. "I'm letting you go and telling you to back off. I know you're used to doing whatever you want, but I'm not Sheriff Malone, and I won't be your lovesick puppy that lets you have free rein."

Standing, I glared at him. "And I'm grateful for that fact."

He glared and stood, grabbing his coat from a rack in the corner and pulling it on. "Jane, I'll be back soon. Show Miss Clark here to the door." He left, slamming the door behind him.

Jane stood and extended her hand. "I'm Jane. You must be Ivy. I recognize you from your picture."

I shook her hand and frowned. "My picture?"

"In Sheriff Malone's office."

I tilted my head and looked around the room. "Isn't this his office?"

"It's through that door," she said, pointing at a closed door.

"I always thought that was a closet."

"He said he doesn't use the office often. Since he didn't have a secretary, it was easier for him to sit out here."

"I see." What picture could he possibly have of me? I'd never given him one.

"Sheriff Malone told me all about you."

I gave her a half-hearted smile. "So I guess you aren't going to let me talk to Livy?"

She smiled and adjusted her glasses. "I'll give you five minutes."

I grinned and went through the door in the back. It led to an area with two cells. Livy was rolled up in a ball on a small bed.

"Livy?" I said.

She sat up. "Ivy! Did you find anything?"

"Not about the murder, but give me time. Do you know anything about Jacob or Noah and drugs?"

She frowned. "No."

"I found some at the camp."

"I've never seen anyone doing drugs there."

"Selling is what I'm thinking."

"Hmm. Noah wants to travel around to different small towns. Could that be why?"

I shrugged. "Maybe. I can't stay. Ledford might come back. Just know I'm working on it."

"Thanks." She smiled slightly. "Did you notice how mad Anton got when Ledford took me?"

I grinned. "Yes. And he insisted on helping me. I don't think he's going to sleep until we get you out."

"I guess I have that."

"Does the TV work?" I asked, pointing at a screen on the wall.

"I haven't tried."

"Ledford won't be happy if he comes and sees me here. Try not to feel bad, alright? We'll figure this out."

"Thanks."

When I got back to the diner, things were quiet. Spring was only a few weeks away, and I hoped that would bring more people in. It had been so empty lately. I worried about people avoiding the diner after Jacob died, but it would be hard to tell since people didn't like to come out in the snow. I went up to my apartment and sat on my recliner. Creepers was curled up on the sofa, sleeping.

Spring being near meant my birthday was even closer. I pulled out my phone to see the date. My eyes went wide. My birthday was in three days. I'd been too busy to notice. Not that birthdays were that exciting. This was one I'd been dreading. I was going to be thirty. At least my life was moving better than it had been a year ago. Now I had Creepers, the diner, and a possible boyfriend. No one here knew when my birthday was, and I wasn't going to bring it up.

The TV sitting in a box against the wall might be nice if I ever figured out how to hook it up. I spend a lot of time sitting and staring out the window when I'm home. Taking time to think is great, but an occasional break would be appreciated. I could go downstairs, but no one down there needed my help. I wasn't sure how long I sat there thinking.

A knock on the door got me up. I opened the door to see Ledford. If this was going to be a regular thing, I wasn't going to be happy about my new door. There were very few people I wanted to see less.

"It's gone," Ledford said.

"The drugs?" I asked.

"Everything. The snow caves have been knocked over, and the tent and everything in it are gone. It looks like a car drove over to where the tent had been."

"What about the people?"

"Some of them are walking around the area, but they aren't saying anything. Noah Cutler is nowhere to be seen. You know that's your fault. If you hadn't gone and poked your nose around, they wouldn't have needed to hide any evidence."

I crossed my arms. "If I hadn't, you wouldn't even know it had been there. You'd already searched, and you already decided Livy was guilty."

"Livy is guilty. That has nothing to do with the drugs. I would have found them, eventually."

Arguing never got me anywhere, so I just shrugged. I doubted he would have gone back.

He pointed at me and frowned. "Don't interfere again. Do you understand?"

I shut the door. I refused to agree to something I wasn't going to do. The corn kids, as Boyd called them, didn't have a car. How would Noah get away so fast? My boots were in the corner. I pulled them on and grabbed my coat. I was going to find Noah, and I was going to figure out who killed Jacob.

When I got to the campsite, no one was there. The only thing to show they had been here was the trampled snow and small mounds that used to be snow caves. A car pulled up behind me, and José got out. He had on a big coat and was carrying a baseball bat.

"What are you doing?" I asked.

"I'm getting to know you pretty well. I watched you go out to your car, and you looked guilty. You're up to something. I figured I better follow you in case you need help."

"What's with the baseball bat?"

He held it up to his shoulder. "We never have a suitable weapon when we need one."

"Look for signs of—well, anything."

I kept my eyes on the ground, not sure what I was looking for. We wandered around for a few minutes, and I wondered if we were wasting time.

"Over here," José called. I rushed over, and he pointed at footprints leading away from the camp. They were big, and there was only one set.

"How did Ledford miss that?" I asked. "He had to have been looking for footprints."

"Should we follow?"

"No."

He raised his brow. "No?"

I grinned. "I'm kidding. You know we're going. Let's only walk on one side so we don't mess the prints up, just in case." We followed the prints until we got to the plowed road. We crossed, and the footprints picked up on the other side.

"This isn't the Smiths' land anymore," José said. "I'm not sure who owns this area."

My toes were cold. Next winter, I was getting better boots. We walked into a grove of trees, and I frowned. "It's going to get dark soon."

"Do you want to come back tomorrow?" José asked.

"No, let's just move fast." The prints went around a clump of trees, and an old log cabin stood in front of us. I stopped in my tracks. "I'm not sure I do creepy old cabins. That might be where I draw the line."

"Someone might live there," he said. "Should we knock?"

I studied the cabin. The roof sagged, and the shutters hadn't been painted in a long time. "I bet it's on someone's land, but no one lives there. Look how run-down it is."

"You're probably right. How would any of those corn kids know it was here, though? It's not an obvious place to come."

I shivered. "No, but a bunch of kids hanging around with nothing to do might wander and find things."

"True. Should we check?"

"What do you think?"

José ran a hand through his black hair. "Let's knock."

We reached the door, and I had a strong feeling it was abandoned. The only footprints in the area went to the door. José tapped on the door, and we waited. I was a lot more scared than I wanted to admit. The person had to be in there unless they had gone out a different way.

A door slammed from the other side of the cabin. José took off around the corner of the house, and I followed. When we got to the back, we saw someone running. I couldn't tell who it was because they had their hood up.

"I've got him. You check the house," José said.

I turned and pulled open the creaky back door. I knew José was more likely to catch someone. He ran on purpose, and I only ran if I was being chased or chasing someone. The cabin didn't have window coverings, so the evening light still shone in. The place showed signs of abandonment. There was no furniture and thick dust on everything. Someone had boarded up a fireplace in the corner.

I went through two empty rooms, but nothing caught my attention. I went back into the main room and looked out the window, hoping to see José. He was walking toward the cabin. It was almost as cold in the cabin as outside. José reached the cabin, breathing deeply.

"I lost them. A big drop goes down to the creek, and he practically threw himself down and ran off. I wasn't willing to break my neck."

I nodded. "I looked around here. There's not a lot." I looked back at the fireplace. A hammer sat next to it and a board. "Could the fireplace be hiding something? I thought the people who left the cabin boarded it up. But it could have been recent."

"It's possible. We should probably tell Ledford. He wouldn't be happy if we uncovered the fireplace and found the drugs. I think we need to let him do it so he won't be mad."

"The hammer isn't dusty," I said, squatting next to it. "I'm worried if we leave, he might come back. If the drugs are in there, he might take them."

"We can call Ledford and wait for him."

I pulled out my phone. "I don't have his number."

"Me neither."

"Court has to be over. I'll call Jett and ask him for it."

I dialed his number and waited.

"Hey, Ivy. How's it going?" he asked.

"Good. How was court?"

"Long. What's up?"

"Can you give me Ledford's number?"

He was quiet for a moment. "You want to call Ledford?"

"Yes."

"Do I want to know why?"

"Nope. You'd be happier just giving me the number."

"Where are you?" he asked.

I squeezed my eyes shut. "In Muddy Creek."

He let out a loud breath. "Where in Muddy Creek?"

"I'm not sure."

"You're at the Smiths' farm, aren't you?"

"No."

"Are you with Boyd?"

"José."

"Could you please just spit out where you are and what you're doing?"

I looked at José. He was grinning.

"You have a lot to think about. Ledford can handle this."

"You think I'm going to sleep if I don't know what you're up to? I know you, Ivy. You're going to get yourself hurt or something."

"We might have found something in a cabin. We want Ledford to come look."

"What cabin?"

"I don't know. It's across the road from the Smiths' farm."

"The Millers own that old thing. It's probably not safe to be in."

"We think there might be drugs boarded up behind the fireplace."

"You think? That sounds really random. Go home so I can sleep knowing you aren't in danger."

I sighed. "Fine."

"Thank you. Call me when you get home."

"Alright. Bye." I hung up. "He's not helpful."

"So we leave?" José asked.

"Yes, but I say we tell Ledford on the way home. We don't want to give anyone time to move things."

Chapter 8

"I want to talk to Miss Clark," a voice boomed through the diner the following morning. I hurried out to see Mayor Jepson standing near the doorway. When he spotted me, he scowled. "Miss Clark, do you really think it's appropriate to have your diner open while an investigation is going on?"

I'm sure my face clouded up. "The investigation isn't about the diner." The two tables of customers were all watching the exchange.

"But it happened in the diner, and the murder suspect worked here."

"She didn't when it happened."

Mayor Jepson rubbed his double chin. "I don't see why that matters. It links her to this place, and this is where it happened. I want it closed until further notice."

"Why?" I asked. "Deputy Ledford already searched it. Any clues would be somewhere else."

His gaze pierced me. "Closed until further notice."

I nodded.

"Mr. Garcia can come in and do the behind-the-scenes things that need doing, but that's all." He turned and stormed from the building. I frowned. Who was Mr. Garcia, and what did he need to do here?

"Finish your food," I told the people at the tables. "I doubt he'll come back to throw you out." They gave me sympathetic glances. All of them were regulars and wouldn't judge me. I went back to the kitchen. José and Anton were frowning.

"I guess you can go," I said.

"That's pretty lame of the mayor," Anton said. "He's just abusing his power. I'm telling you, Boyd should run against him. I bet he would win."

"I doubt he knows how to be the mayor."

"He could learn."

"Who is Mr. Garcia?" I asked. "An inspector or something?"

José chuckled. "I would guess that's me."

Anton laughed. "I didn't know you had a last name."

I shook my head. "Neither did I, and I sign the paychecks. Sorry, José." José was one of my best friends, and I'd never even wondered if he had a last name.

José grinned. "So you all thought I was cool enough to be like Madonna or Zendaya? I'll take that as a compliment."

The door opened, and Hannah entered. Her eyes were puffy and red. That seemed to be her permanent state. Either she was an emotional person or she'd had a bad week. Possibly both.

"I'm sorry, the mayor said we have to close," I told her.

She nodded. "Any chance I can get a dessert to go? I can pay."

I felt bad for the girl, so I nodded. She followed me into the kitchen, and I handed her a large cookie. She handed me a dollar, which was low, but that was fine.

"Thanks. Everything is so stressful." Her hands shook as she took a big bite.

"Are you staying in town?" I asked. José and Anton were cleaning, but I could tell they were listening.

"I got a room at the bed-and-breakfast down the street. Most of us are packed in here. We have to share rooms. The deputy still won't let us leave town. I don't know why. They already know Livy did it."

"They must not be positive if they're keeping you here."

She bit the cookie again. "This is all a mess. If Jacob would have stayed out of everything, there wouldn't have been a problem. He drove Livy to it. I feel bad for her."

"What do you mean?" I asked. Anton looked like he wanted to say something, so I shook my head slightly.

Hannah seemed to be in the mood to talk, and she might know things.

"Jacob had a thing for Livy. He was always following her around and trying to get her attention. She hated it. She couldn't have a moment to herself. Every time she sat down, he sat next to her."

"There had to be other people who didn't like him."

"No one liked him. It was almost like he tried to take over Noah's life. He inserted himself into our group and started dressing like Noah and talking like him. It was almost creepy, like there were two Noahs. He talked more and more, and Noah got quiet. Once he took over, his true personality came out."

"And what was that?" I asked.

"He was like a terrible boss. Everyone had to do what he said, or he freaked out. I felt bad for Noah. Jacob ruined his dream. Now, everything has fallen apart. I need to go. Can I have another cookie?"

"Take as many as you want." We weren't going to need them. She grabbed a handful.

"Thanks. I don't have any money to eat."

"How are you paying for the bed-and-breakfast?"

"Deputy Ledford is paying for that."

José handed her a to-go container full of food.

"Thanks!" She rushed from the diner like we might change our minds.

"That was odd," José said. "Did you see how she was shaking?"

"Yeah, she was upset."

"Or she was coming off something."

"Like what?"

"Drugs, maybe."

"Do you think so?"

José shrugged. "It's just a guess. If she's not eating, that might be it, although I figure the name bed-and-breakfast means they serve at least breakfast."

I drummed my fingers against my leg. "I'm going to tell Ledford he needs to make sure they all have food over there. If the city is paying for the B&B, I bet they would pay for meals. Are you two alright cleaning up?"

"Yep," José said. "We'll close up, and I'll finish today's paperwork."

I grabbed my coat and headed to the sheriff's office. These things were a lot more pleasant when I worked with Jett. Not that he usually wanted my help, but he wasn't annoying like Ledford. He'd been livid when we'd stopped last night and told him about the cabin.

Jane sat at the front desk, and Ledford's desk was empty.

"Hi, Jane," I said. "Is Deputy Ledford in?"

She shook her head. "He hasn't come in today."

"Can I talk to Livy?"

"Sure thing."

"Thanks." I opened the door to the area with the cells and found Livy in almost the same position as yesterday. The TV was on, and she was watching a game show. She sat up when I entered.

"How's it going?" I asked.

She shrugged. "Nothing to report."

"That's a nice blanket," I said, pointing at a large patchwork quilt.

"My mom brought it."

I stepped forward and held the bars. "I just talked to Hannah. She said Jacob had a crush on you or something like that."

Livy frowned. "Really? I doubt it. Jacob ignored me most of the time. Noah was the one who annoyed me. He's dating Hannah, but he always follows me around and touches my hair. It made Hannah crazy. I tried to stay away from him, but he can be persistent."

I rubbed my lips together. "Why would Hannah lie about that? Do you think Hannah would do drugs?"

Livy shrugged. "Maybe. I've never seen her. She's passed out drunk before, though. It made Noah really mad. He gave her a huge lecture the next day. They had a colossal screaming fight. That was before we came here. I haven't seen her drink since we set up the camp."

I nodded and held out a bag of cookies. She stood and came to take it. I probably should have gotten permission. Many things in Muddy Creek were different from other places I'd gone. They didn't even check people for weapons when they came to visit prisoners. They needed a bigger staff to make things run more smoothly.

I left Livy and went to talk to Jane. "Do you know when Ledford will be in?"

She shook her head. "He should have been in over an hour ago. I tried to call him, but it went to voicemail."

A chill ran over my body. Had Ledford gone to the cabin last night? What if something had happened? I wanted to call Jett, but he would be in the middle of a trial and wouldn't answer. Even if he did, he was far away. I called anyway.

I dialed his number as I rushed to the diner, but it went to voicemail. I stopped to leave a quick message. "Hey, Jett. It's Ivy. Ledford didn't come in this morning. I'm worried he might've gone to the cabin. I don't know who to tell. I'll try to find him."

I hung up and ran the rest of the way. Boyd stood outside the diner. He pointed at the Closed sign. "What's with that?"

"The mayor made us close. Get in the car." I climbed into my car, and Boyd got in the passenger seat.

"What's happening?" he asked as we pulled out.

"Ledford didn't show up at work today. I'm worried something happened to him."

Boyd chuckled. "We're worried about Ledford now? That sounds desperate."

I glanced at him. "I don't like Ledford, but that doesn't mean I want anything to happen to him."

"Are we just driving around, hoping to find him?"

I quickly caught him up on everything from the night before. "I want to go look at the cabin. I probably should have asked you before I made you come."

"You know I would come."

I did know. Boyd was dependable. "I called Jett. I probably shouldn't have, but it's hard when we don't have a lot of law out here. We probably should have taken José and Anton."

When we pulled up by the Smiths' farm, we saw Ledford's patrol car on the opposite side. He must have gone to the cabin. We got out, and I grabbed my pepper spray and put my key in my pocket and my purse under the seat.

Ledford's prints in the snow went the same way as José's and mine from the night before. Ours went two directions, but Ledford's only went one.

"Maybe he came this morning instead of last night," I said hopefully. It hadn't snowed overnight, so we couldn't tell by looking at his car. We hurried through the field and into the trees. We paused when we got to the cabin.

"The Millers own this," Boyd said. "I remember coming here when I was young. It's looking worn down. They must not use it anymore."

"What should we do?" I wondered. "I could go in, and you could wait out here in case something happens."

He lifted his brow. "How would I know something happened? Let's just go in."

I turned the doorknob, and we let ourselves in. I led Boyd to the large room with the fireplace. Ledford lay on the floor with his back to us. Ropes bound his hands behind him, and his feet and legs were tied.

We rushed to his side, and he turned his head. Relief flooded his eyes as we bent over him. I pulled a handkerchief from his mouth, and he swallowed.

"I never thought I would be glad to see you, Miss Clark," he said with a raspy voice.

I smiled. "You know I can't let anything go."

Boyd pulled a pocketknife from his coat pocket and began sawing at the ropes around Ledford's wrists.

"I wish you'd come last night," he said. "I feel like I've been here forever."

"Did you see who did this?"

He shook his head. "I pulled the boards from the fireplace. You were right. There were thousands of dollars of cocaine and heroin. Someone attacked me from behind. I don't know what happened, but I woke up tied here."

I looked at the fireplace. "It looks like whoever it was didn't take the drugs."

The ropes on his hands fell to the floor, and he pushed himself into a sitting position. He held out his hand, and Boyd handed him the knife. He sawed at the ropes on his legs. "It sounded like someone was boarding up the back door when I woke up, but I couldn't get up to see what was happening."

"There's some dry blood on the back of your head," I said. "Nothing fresh." There was blood on the floor, but not enough to cause concern.

"I feel awful," he said. "I can't hardly see straight." The ropes on his legs came off, and he started on his ankles.

Boyd went to the door and pushed on it. It wouldn't open. "Why board up the back door but leave the front door unlocked?"

"Because we can't do everything at once," a voice from behind said. I spun around to see a man holding a gun. He had covered his face in a ski mask, but I was almost positive it was Noah. Ledford had gotten all his ropes off, but he didn't look in any condition to fight, especially against someone with a gun.

"Sit down," the man said. Boyd sat near Ledford, and I sat by Boyd. My pepper spray wouldn't do any good from this distance. Hammering began behind me, and I turned. Another man in a mask was putting a board over the window.

"Just sit tight, and we'll have you all boarded in. Put everything in your pockets on the floor in front of you." I pulled out the pepper spray, my key, and my phone.

I looked around for a weapon and wished I had José's baseball bat. If he came close enough, I could spray him. But I guessed he wouldn't do that. Ledford looked like he might puke, and Boyd just stared at the man. If they boarded us in and left, that would be alright. It would be annoying to get the boards down, but we could do it.

I heard more hammering from the front. That meant there were at least three people we would have to deal with.

My phone rang, and I cringed.

"Toss me your phone," the man said.

I slid it across the floor.

He picked it up and looked at the screen. "Jett Malone. Isn't that the sheriff?"

"He'll come if he thinks something's wrong or if I don't answer."

He slid the phone back. "Answer it and tell him you're fine. Put it on speakerphone."

I pushed the button and held it to my ear. "Hello, Sheriff Malone." I hadn't called him Sheriff Malone since the first week I met him.

There was a pause. "Ivy? Are you alright?"

"Of course, Sheriff."

Another pause. "Are you with anyone?"

"Boyd and Ledford."

"Am I on speaker? Can you hear me, Ledford?"

"Yes. Hey, Jett."

My heart was pounding. Ledford would never call him Jett. With luck, Jett would sense we were in trouble.

"Can I give you a job?" Jett asked. Ledford was holding his head and had his eyes squeezed shut.

"I don't think so," I said. "Deputy Ledford has a monstrous headache."

"Do I hear hammering? Are you at the diner?"

I looked at the man with the gun. He nodded.

"Yes."

"I thought all the construction on the diner was finished."

"I guess they needed to come do some things to the windows."

"Do you have to pay more? How many workers did they send?"

"I haven't looked. Maybe three."

"Nice. I have to drive to another city, and I'm not looking forward to it. Will you stay on the phone with me? I'd rather you didn't have me on speakerphone, though. I don't need Boyd and Ledford listening."

The masked man shook his head.

"I can't. My phone is stuck on speakerphone." I rolled my eyes. Improvising can be rough.

"That's weird."

The sounds coming from his phone sounded like he was in the car. I hoped he was coming this way. Now, the window was completely boarded up, and I could hear multiple hammers in the front.

"Ledford?" Jett said.

I looked over at Ledford. He was lying down with his eyes closed but breathing deeply.

"He's taking a nap," I said.

"At the diner?"

Boyd frowned. "You know Ledford. He can sleep any-where. He might need time off."

"I'm going to hang up. I just remembered someone I needed to call."

"See you." The phone went dead. I hoped Jett had realized we were in trouble. I was almost sure he had.

Chapter 9

We sat silently for thirty minutes. The man with the gun should be getting tired. He'd been pointing the gun at us for a long time. The hammering was still going on. They would have us completely boarded in soon. I hoped Ledford was okay. He hadn't woken up. He must have a concussion.

"Is there a bathroom in here?" I asked.

The man shifted. "There is, but there isn't any running water."

"I don't care. I'm getting desperate. I had two mugs of cocoa this morning."

"I'll take you." He looked at Boyd. "You come." Boyd stood, and the man motioned forward. We walked in front of him down a short hall and into a horrible-smelling bathroom. I wrinkled my nose. Spiderwebs filled the windowsill, and there was a thick layer of dust. I'd seen it yesterday, but I hadn't taken a lot of notice of its condition.

"Hurry," the man said.

I began closing the door, but he stopped it. "Leave it open."

"No."

"Leave it open, or hold it."

I stepped closer to the toilet and heard a loud crack, and Boyd let out a yell. His foot had broken through the rotted floor. The man turned to see what was happening, and I grabbed the ceramic lid of the toilet tank and swung it at his arm in one swift motion.

The man yelled, and the gun fell to the floor. I bent to grab it, but Boyd snatched it and pointed it at the man.

The man held his arm and glared at me. I swung the lid again and hit his shoulder, knocking him over. He rolled, jumped to his feet, and ran. I looked from Boyd to the man. I could tell Boyd was in pain. The front door opened and slammed shut. Boyd put the gun on the floor and tried to extract his leg from the wooden planks.

Leaning down, I took Boyd's hands and helped him pull his leg free. His pants were torn, and his knee was bleeding.

"I'm fine," he said. "We need to get out of here." I put his arm over my shoulders and helped him walk back to Ledford. The hammering hadn't stopped. They must be finishing with the front door. Weren't they worried we might shoot them?

Boyd sat on the ground and pulled on the hole in his pants until it ripped more and exposed his wound. I handed him one of my gloves, and he held it over the gash.

"Ledford?" I said. I shook his shoulder, but he didn't wake.

"I'm going to need a few stitches," Boyd said.

"Sorry. It wouldn't have happened if I hadn't had him take me to the bathroom."

Boyd chuckled. "I grew up on a farm. I collect scars."

The hammering stopped, and I looked in that direction. "Do you think they all have guns?"

Boyd kept the glove pressed to his knee. "No. I bet this gun belongs to Ledford."

"Do you think they'll leave?"

"Not sure. The drugs are still here. I imagine that's the only reason they're still around."

My phone rang, and I picked it up. "Jett?"

"Am I on speakerphone?" he asked.

"No. We're boarded in the cabin. I bet we can get out, but Ledford's unconscious and Boyd's leg is hurt."

"I'm here. I just need to walk from my truck. Is anyone in the cabin with you?"

"No, they just left. You might run into them if they go to the road."

"Are they armed?"

"I don't know. One had a gun, but we took it. I don't know about the others."

"I'm coming."

"Be careful." I put my phone in my pocket. "Jett's almost here."

Boyd nodded. "Can I have your other glove?" I handed it to him, and he pressed it to his injury. I went to the front of the house and pulled on the door. It opened, but boards were going across the opening. I assumed they hadn't done the best job on this door since they knew we had the gun, and it was the last door they boarded.

I peeked out of a crack in the boards and saw Jett jogging toward us. He had a crowbar in one hand and his gun in the other.

"Ivy?" he called when he got to the door.

"I'm here."

"Stand back."

I moved out of the way and waited as he pried the boards off the entrance. Boyd came limping over, and we watched. I thought about helping, but I didn't have a tool, and he was going fast. There was a siren in the distance.

"What's that?" I asked.

"I called an ambulance after I talked to you. I wasn't sure what was happening, but when you said Ledford was taking a nap, I figured I should play it safe."

"I hoped you could understand we were in trouble."

"I figured as soon as you said Sheriff Malone. And Ledford never calls me Jett. It was all too weird to be normal. Can you run to the road and flag down the ambulance? I told them to look for my truck, but there's no good road, and it's snowy, so they won't know where to come."

Stepping through the gap in the boards, I took off for the road. I couldn't see any prints from our capturers. They must have gone farther into the trees. That might make them easy to catch. I saw the ambulance driving slowly over the snowy surface when I got to the road. I waved my arms and forced myself not to hold my side. I hate running, but I should probably keep up the practice with José if I'm going to keep finding myself in these situations.

The paramedics put Ledford into the ambulance, and Boyd went with them just to be safe. Jett made a few calls, then we walked through the trees.

"Sorry you had to come."

Jett carried a bag full of the drugs. I couldn't believe they hadn't grabbed them. He shook his head and smiled. "I'm just surprised it wasn't the middle of the night. That's when I usually get those calls from you."

It was true. I'd woken him up plenty since I'd moved here for one thing or another. "Will you get in trouble for not being in court?"

"The judge was understanding. The trial's a big mess, so I think he was glad to have a reason for a break."

We came from under the tree covering, and my mouth turned down. "Can you see my car?"

"Nope. It was right in front of my truck."

I searched my pockets. "The man made us put everything on the floor. He must have taken my key."

Jett rubbed his eyes. "We need more help in Muddy Creek. At least two more officers."

We walked to his car and got in. "I didn't see any of their prints coming this way."

"They must have circled around. Did you recognize any of them?"

I shook my head. "They had masks. I think the one who held the gun on us was Noah, but I'm not one hundred percent sure."

"I'll take you back to town before I go after them."

"Won't that make you lose them?"

Jett sighed. "I'll make a call to Wichita. If they go that way and stay on the road, the police will catch them. If they didn't go that way, we should catch them on the way to town." He stared ahead as he drove, and I watched him. His eye was twitching on the side.

"Are you okay?" I asked.

He was quiet for a minute. I hoped he wasn't secretly mad at me for coming here. "I'm fine."

"Liar."

He gripped the steering wheel and let out a slow breath. "I don't know, Ivs. I'm trying."

"What can I do?" I asked, feeling a lump in my throat.

"I'm just so tired. Things have been nonstop for the past few months, and I never have time to stop and process anything. I feel like I'm barely holding myself together sometimes."

"Part of that's my fault."

"No. It's not your fault everything has happened the way it has. You might have dug a few cases up, but they needed to come to light. Even when I have time to sleep, I'm struggling. I try to ignore the fact that I have no time for myself, but it's taking a toll."

"You need a vacation."

"Probably. I took that week in January, but that didn't go as planned."

Jett had used his vacation to do security for a wealthy family, and it had ended in a murder. It had been the week he finally kissed me, and he hadn't since then.

"You need to go somewhere and just relax."

"I can't. Not unless we get more officers. Ledford should have had a partner to back him up last night. That's how it's supposed to work."

"I wish I could help."

"I'm fine. As soon as I get a good night's sleep, I'll be great."

"Are you sure?"

He kept his eyes ahead. "Probably. It's hard to work all day and some nights, then go home to an empty house, then do it all again the next day. I don't even have a dog. I don't even have a goldfish."

I smiled. "Do you want a dog?"

"I don't have time for a dog. Dogs need attention. I'm feeling more like a machine and less like a person."

"What if you did a dog share with Boyd?"

A small smile came to his lips. "A dog share?"

"Boyd could watch it during the day, then you could take it home at night. Boyd loves animals. Creepers likes him more than he likes me."

"My schedule is too unpredictable."

"You can take Creepers anytime you want."

He turned and gave me a tired smile. "I mean this in the nicest way. There are cat people, and there are dog people."

"And you're a dog person?"

"Yep. Creepers is cute and all, but I only pay attention to him to impress you."

I grinned. "I've kind of wondered about that. When you pet him, you're a little stiff."

"Dogs are predictable. Cats? Never. They might cuddle up to you one second, then rip off your face the next. They make me nervous."

I laughed. "You don't have to pet my cat."

"I'm getting used to him. He's mellow for a cat."

"Why don't you come to the diner, and I'll warm something up for you. The mayor closed us down for now, but the fridge still has some things."

"Why did he shut you down?"

"Because Livy used to work there."

"That makes no sense."

"No, but it's fine. We aren't busy when it's cold, anyway."

"I better not. I need to make some more calls and see if the trial tomorrow can be put off. Looking for the people who captured you should also be a priority, but my guess is they'll get caught on the way to Wichita. I don't want to leave Muddy Creek with no law, and who knows when Ledford will be back."

"It should be a rule that they have to send more officers to work here."

"It would be ideal, but no one wants to come here. The pay isn't competitive, and it's a small town. That doesn't draw people in."

We pulled into town, and Jett stopped in front of the diner. "Be careful, and I'll see you around."

I nodded and climbed out. I went to the door, unsure of my own feelings. Jett hadn't even hugged me. He had admitted to petting Creepers to get my attention, but it seemed weird he hadn't even tried to kiss me in over a month. I watched his Cybertruck drive away. It was the most ridiculous vehicle I'd ever seen. But he was impressed with it.

I looked up and saw Creepers sitting in the upstairs window. José had helped set up my TV the other day, so after a shower, I wore my pajamas for the rest of the day and sat with Creepers to watch a movie. I needed time to stop and think before I could help Livy.

Chapter 10

The following morning, I looked out the window and saw my car in the diner lot. I grabbed my phone to see a text from Jett. It said, "Hey, Ivy. The police in Wichita caught two people with your car. They were two of the kids from the commune. The third one wasn't in the car and hasn't been found. I put your key under your welcome mat."

I sighed. That meant one of our capturers was still out there. It also meant Jett hadn't gotten a good night's sleep again.

My phone pinged. It was Jett again. In his text, he mentioned Ledford suffered a concussion but was recovering, and José was on his way to collect Boyd, who had ten stitches in his knee.

The leftovers in the fridge would go bad, so I loaded them into bags and took them to the B&B. A woman with short gray hair greeted me when I knocked.

"Hi, I'm Ivy Clark from the diner?"

The woman nodded. "I've seen you around. I'm Miss Medley."

"I brought some leftovers. I thought maybe some of the college kids might want them."

She rolled her eyes. "Why does everyone refer to them as the college kids? They're all dropouts and as annoying as middle schoolers. They're going to ruin my entire place." She grabbed the bags from my hand.

"Can I help with anything?"

"No." She shut the door, and I stood there for a moment.

"She's not a people person," someone said from the walkway. I turned and saw Carlos. He had on a large coat and gloves. "I'm wandering the town just to stay away from her."

I walked down the steps and put my icy hands in my pockets. "How are you all holding up?"

"Better than when we were living in the snow. The sheriff came by this morning. I guess some of our group got arrested for something yesterday."

"Do you know who?"

"He didn't say, but I know who isn't here. Josh, Pat, and Noah."

I nodded. I knew it was Noah.

"He didn't say what they did, but I can't say I'm surprised."

"Why?"

"They're just the type, you know? I bet Noah's into a bunch of illegal stuff."

"Like what?"

"Who knows? But nothing would shock me."

"How's Hannah?"

He shook his head. "That girl has issues. She's having some terrible withdrawal from something. She tried to bribe me to go find her drugs. Can you believe that? Do I look like someone who knows where to get drugs? She's been trying to get everyone to get her something. I gave her a lecture about taking care of your body, and she spit at me."

"Hmm. Someone should get her some help."

"I was going to talk to that Ledford dude, but he hasn't been back since he put everyone here. When the sheriff came, I was going to tell him, but he looks like he has enough problems."

"He looked tired?"

He ran his hand over his black hair. "Yeah, and he looked about three seconds away from yelling at everyone."

"I better go. Will you come tell me if anything weird happens?"

He shrugged. "Sure."

When I got to the diner, Jett stood out front with Livy.

"Hey," I said, meeting them.

"Can Livy stay with you?" Jett asked. "I'm not keeping her locked up until we have more evidence, and we know that isn't going to happen since she didn't do it."

"You believe me?" Livy asked.

Jett nodded. "Of course. I've known you forever. My guess is on Noah. I pulled up some files on him, and he's been in trouble more than once. He's also the one person who hasn't been found. If nothing else, he's behind the drugs."

"Can't Livy stay with her parents?"

Livy frowned. "They can't take it. They're really stressed. I think it would be better to let them pretend it's not happening until you find the actual killer."

"You mean I find the actual killer," Jett said.

Livy smiled. "My money's on Ivy."

I put my hand on her arm. "You're welcome to stay with me. Let's go around the back. I'm trying to make it feel like my diner life and my apartment are two separate places." We walked around back and up the stairs to my door. I unlocked it, and we went in.

Jett looked around the sitting room. "Wow, it's cute."

I tilted my head. "Cute?"

He grinned. "That was the first word that came to mind. I like the fireplace."

"I'm going to go lie down," Livy said. "I'm getting a headache."

"Alright. I left your stuff in there. Let me know if you need anything."

"Thanks." She turned and disappeared into the guest room.

"Come see the kitchen," I said, leading Jett from the room. I'd wanted to show him all the new space since it was finished but hadn't had the chance. I flipped on the light and smiled.

"Nice," he said. "It must feel cozy after cooking in the diner."

I nodded. The area wasn't huge, but I already loved it. It had a double stainless steel oven. I wasn't sure why I wanted that. I didn't need two for just myself, but now I could cook two things at once. My table was small with only four chairs, but so far, I'd only used one, anyway. It had a purple tablecloth that matched the lavender curtains.

"Have you tried out your ovens yet?" he asked.

"Of course. I made cookies, and I used both ovens just to make sure they worked. The diner ovens cook hotter and more evenly, but these are pretty good."

Jett opened the freezer, and I cringed. "Four kinds of ice cream?"

"You never know when you might need a variety."

He shut it. "I have at least six in mine. But they are all hard with freezer burn. Is the apartment Creepers approved?"

"Yep. He still prefers sitting on the windowsill in my room, but he wanders out occasionally."

"Do you have any fun plans tomorrow?"

My heart pounded. Was he going to ask me on a date? Probably not. He still had court hearings. I wondered if he knew tomorrow was my birthday. "No. I think I'll go talk to Hannah again."

"She's one of the corn kids?"

"Yeah."

"I'm having a hard time wrapping my mind around this case since Ledford's been working it."

"And you don't sleep."

"That too."

"Hannah is Noah's girlfriend. I think. Livy says they're off and on. I think she might be going through a drug withdrawal."

"I wonder if Noah was getting it for her. He must be dealing. There was so much in that fireplace it couldn't be for one person."

"That's what I was thinking."

Jett scratched his chin. "I should probably go talk to Hannah. I wanted to leave this to Ledford, but who knows how long it will take until he feels better."

"But you have to go to court."

"I just got a call a half hour ago. They rescheduled the trial for next month."

"Is that good or bad?"

He sighed and ran a hand through his brown hair. "It depends. I want to get it behind me, but I really need a break."

"Trying to solve a murder won't be a break."

He nodded. "I know." His phone chimed, and he glanced down at it. "It's Ledford. He said he's on his way home and ready to work tomorrow."

"How long does it take to heal from a concussion?"

"Longer than two days. I better go. Jane is still training on some things, and I need to help her."

"Alright." I walked him to the door and pulled it open. "See you."

"Bye." He took the stairs two at a time, and I blew out a breath as I watched him. He hadn't even pretended to want to kiss me. It was fine. Fine, fine, fine. It wasn't fine, but I couldn't really do anything about it.

I went looking for Creepers. I poured some cat food into his bowl, and he came running from wherever he'd been hiding. Sitting on the floor, I watched him eat.

There was a knock on the door. I reluctantly stood and answered. José stood there.

"I have Boyd in my car," José said. "I know Jett said that Livy's already staying here, but can Boyd stay on your couch? He can't move too much and won't be able to ride his bike into town for a while."

"Don't you have a house?"

José grinned. "Yeah, but can you really imagine me babysitting Boyd? Besides, a skunk got into the basement, so I've been staying away as much as I can."

I shook my head. "He can stay on the couch. Will he be able to walk up the stairs?"

"If he takes it slow."

I waited for José to help Boyd up and into the apartment. He was limping, but he looked happy.

"Thanks, Ivy," he said. He sank onto the couch and caught his breath. "That's a lot of stairs."

"You wanna watch a movie?" I asked. "I can make popcorn."

"Sure," Boyd said. "It's been a while since I've watched a movie with anyone."

Guilt overwhelmed me. I counted Boyd as a friend, but we never did fun things together.

"You can stay if you want," I told José. I was sure he would decline, but he agreed and sat by Boyd. I handed the remote to Boyd. "You two choose a movie, and I'll make the popcorn."

As soon as the smell of popcorn filled the air, Livy came into the kitchen. "Are you making popcorn?"

"Yes. Boyd, José, and I are going to watch a movie. Do you want to join us?"

She rubbed her temples. "I think I might."

"Boyd's choosing, so there's no telling what it will be."

I handed the bowl to Livy, and we went back to the sitting room.

"Oh no! It's black and white!" Livy said.

Boyd laughed. "Give it a chance."

"I already hate it," Livy said, sitting next to José. I sat on the recliner. Creepers wandered in and jumped on Boyd's lap.

"If I watch this, I get to choose next," Livy said.

"Deal," Boyd agreed.

"Don't I get a say?" José asked. "We should vote or something."

"I doubt we'll ever come to an agreement," Boyd said. "It's better to take turns and suffer through the other's choices."

I sighed. It might turn out to be a long night.

Chapter 11

When the third movie started, I couldn't take it anymore. These three were terrible at picking movies. I hadn't spent a day watching movies in a long time, and I was having trouble paying attention. All I was thinking about was Jett and what he was thinking about me. I needed to know, and I was going to ask.

"I'm going for a walk," I told them. "My legs need to stretch." I put my coat on and walked to the sheriff's office. The sun was beginning to set, so he might have gone home. When I was almost there, I paused. I thought I saw something from the corner of my eye go over the building.

I walked around the building with my eyes on the roof. On the backside of the roof, a figure in black was on their hands and knees, dumping something into a vent. I frowned. That couldn't be good. Someone had positioned a ladder next to the building. I grabbed it and laid it down flat, then I hurried around the corner to the front door.

There was no telling what the person was dumping into the office, so I took a deep breath and entered. Jane wasn't there, so I rushed into Jett's office. His elbows sat on his desk, and he rested his head in his hands. I wasn't good at holding my breath, and I was going to have to breathe soon.

Grabbing Jett's arm, I pulled. He looked up, his eyes not quite focused. After another tug, he stood. I pulled him out of the room and outside away from the office. I took a deep breath, and he fell to his knees.

He blinked. "What are you doing, Ivy? I'm so tired."

"Someone is on the office roof. He was pouring something into a vent."

"Okay. I'll rest for a minute and then deal with it."

I took a deep breath. I stood and ran back around the building. The person in black was hanging from the roof, about to drop. His feet dangled five feet above the ground. As soon as he let go, I charged forward. He landed in a squat, and as soon as he stood, I plowed into him, taking us both down to the hard snow. I grabbed his mask and ripped it off. Noah stared up at me. Not a surprise.

"Get off!" he yelled. He shoved me onto the ground, and I jumped up. He tried to stand, and I kicked him in the chest, knocking him back to the ground. Jett staggered around the corner and looked confused. He pulled his gun out and aimed it at Noah. I wasn't sure how able Jett was, so I watched Noah closely and moved farther away.

Noah raised his arms and glared. "Selling a few drugs doesn't hurt anyone!" he said. "I don't see why you couldn't just mind your businesses. I need that money!"

"Do you really think we left those drugs inside the sheriff's office for you to come grab?" Jett asked. "Those drugs are long gone."

Noah's head and arms fell. "You don't understand."

"What did you do up there?"

He shrugged. "Nothing that bad. I just wanted to get my stuff back."

I thought about calling Ledford to see if he was back, but adding a guy with a concussion probably wasn't the best idea. I didn't want Jett to get close to Noah because Jett wasn't at his best. Noah couldn't be put in a cell because we didn't know what he'd poured inside.

Jett shook his head, and I could see his eyes clearing. He moved closer to Noah and told him to turn around and put his hands together. I watched Jett expertly handcuff Noah without dropping his gun. He grabbed him by the arm and led him away from the building. I followed, still not sure Jett was okay.

My eyes narrowed when Jett walked up to the diner.

"What are you doing?" I asked.

"I have to put him somewhere while I air out the sheriff's office."

"But my diner?"

He sighed. "I don't have any other ideas."

I hurried ahead and unlocked the door. Jett pushed Noah through. When we got inside, he made Noah sit under one of the tables. He took another pair of handcuffs out and cuffed him to the metal table leg that was hooked to the floor.

"I'm not going to sleep knowing he's there," I said.

Jett nodded. "I'll go air out my office and see if I can figure out what he dumped in there. Or I suppose he could tell me." Jett squatted and looked at Noah.

"It wasn't anything dangerous. Just essential oils. They wouldn't knock you out or anything, just make you tired. You never go home. I thought I could make you tired enough to want to leave. It won't even smell by now. If you don't believe me, I left my stuff on the roof when the ladder fell."

"You thought you could find a vent going into the office, dump oil in, and it would make me so tired I would leave? That's the dumbest thing I've heard in a while. I bet the smell didn't even make it into the office." Jett grabbed my hand and pulled me from the diner. He slammed the door, and I locked it.

"I still want to air the office out," he said. "Just to be sure. I can't believe I was almost taken out by essential oils."

"You haven't been sleeping. I'm going to text José and tell him what's happening. I don't want him to hear noises and go down to the diner and find Noah."

Jett frowned. "Why would he hear anything?"

"He's in my apartment watching movies with Livy and Boyd." I sent a quick text, and we went back to his office. We propped the ladder back up, and I tried to convince Jett to let me go up. I didn't think he was stable enough, but he insisted on going.

He was back down in a minute with a grocery bag. "It's essential oils," he said. "That's almost embarrassing. I'm not sure they could really do anything. Especially if he was just dumping them in some random thing up there."

"How much sleep did you get last night?"

"An hour or two."

"You need to take care of yourself."

He rubbed a hand over his face. "I have so much to do, and sleep isn't coming easy."

"Let's go get Noah, put him in a cell, and then you go home and go to bed. You're going to make mistakes if you go on like this."

He yawned. "You're probably right."

It took us twenty minutes to get Noah into a cell for the night. Jett didn't ask any questions. I figured he was almost too tired to even know what was happening. He followed me back to my place so I could drive him home. He didn't live far, but he was stumbling.

"Let me go up and check on the others," I said. He followed me up the back steps and into the front room. José, Livy, and Boyd were still watching TV.

Boyd glanced up at Jett. "You look awful. When's the last time you slept?"

Jett shrugged and sank down into the recliner. Great. Now, I was going to have to get him up. He did look exhausted. His eyes were red and a little puffy.

He yawned, and I heard his jaw crack.

"What have you two been up to?" Boyd asked.

"Arresting people and stuff," Jett said.

"Who are you arresting?" José asked.

"Noah. He was on the roof of my office doing something." He yawned again. "What are you watching?"

"*Casablanca*," Boyd said. "We're giving Livy some culture."

"It's torture," Livy said.

Jett's watch beeped, and he gave a small smile and pushed a button.

"What does that mean?" Boyd asked.

Jett leaned forward and grabbed my hand, then pulled me over next to him. "It means I'm no longer on duty. Now I'm just on call." He looked up at me. "Let's watch a movie." He pulled me onto his lap and wrapped his arms around me, resting them on my stomach.

"You need to go to bed, not watch a movie." I leaned my head against his shoulder and looked at the TV, too aware of all the eyes on me. For once, José and Boyd didn't comment.

"I know what I need," Jett said, rubbing his face against my neck. A chill ran down my arms, and I rested my hands on his. Within two minutes, Jett was breathing deeply, and I was stuck. If I had to be stuck, this was the place I would choose, but I was going to get uncomfortable fast.

Jett let out a loud snore, and we all laughed. He didn't wake up.

"Poor guy," José said. "He really needs more time off."

I tried to move, but he had a good grip on me. "I'm going to get a cramp in my neck, and my back already hurts."

José came over and bent down to recline the chair. It helped a little, but I was still going to be sore if I didn't move soon.

"Can we at least watch a good movie?" I asked.

"I've been watching too much today," Livy said. "I feel gross. I'm going to bed." Standing, she stretched and went into the other room.

"Let's start the movie over so Ivy can see the entire thing," Boyd said.

"No!" I protested. "It's fine where it is."

I tried to reposition myself so my back was slightly against the armrest. That was a little better. I turned my head and stared at Jett. I forced myself to keep my hand where it was and not run it over his cheek and wake him. That was one of the last thoughts I remembered having.

The following morning, I woke to the smell of bacon. Sitting up in my bed, I frowned. I didn't remember coming in here. I wandered into the living room to see Boyd asleep on the couch and José curled up on the floor. Following the smell to the kitchen, I entered to see Jett at the stove, frying bacon.

He grinned. "Morning."

"Good morning," I said. He looked better. His eyes weren't even red. "It was like a big sleepover last night. I can't believe José is asleep on the floor."

"It cracked me up last night when I woke up and saw everyone sleeping. You were hogging the chair, so I threw you in your bed. I hope that's okay."

"I wondered how I got there."

"You were out. I had the best sleep I've had in weeks. That's a nice recliner you've got."

I nodded. "Maybe you need a new bed."

"My mattress isn't that old. My parents gave it to me when I graduated."

"From the academy?"

He grinned. "No, from middle school."

"That was like twenty years ago! Get a new mattress."

"I probably should."

"You didn't need to make breakfast."

"I'm feeling great today. I might as well."

Today was my birthday. I was going to pretend Jett knew and was doing it to be nice. I could have told my friends, but I didn't want them to make a big deal.

José stumbled into the kitchen. "I'm too old to sleep on the floor. I need some routine in my life. We should beg the mayor to let us open."

Jett handed him a plate of eggs and bacon and gave one to me. I sat down at the table and took a bite. "Not bad. If you ever need a job, I might hire you."

He grinned. "I'll keep that in mind. I should probably take some over to Noah. Miss Medley usually takes meals to the prisoners, but I never told her we had one."

"My knee is stiff!" Boyd called from the other room. "Someone needs to help me stand and move a little."

José chuckled. "I'll go."

Chapter 12

The morning flew by, and soon, I was sitting at my table with José, Boyd, and Livy, eating lunch. Jett had left right after breakfast, and the rest of us were brainstorming. We weren't getting very far.

"I still think the murderer has to be Noah," Boyd said. "He was trying to take out Jett."

I shook my head. "Yes, but he was only trying to make him tired, and he used essential oils. That doesn't scream 'killer' to me."

"But he's obviously behind the drugs," José said. "That could have motivated him to kill Jacob if Jacob was messing with his plans."

I picked up my sandwich and took a bite. Even the sandwiches José made were delicious.

Livy picked at her crust. "I'm embarrassed I got involved with any of it."

The doorbell rang, and I got up to open the door. A deliveryman stood there holding a bouquet of red roses in a glass vase. "Ivy Clark?"

"Yes."

He handed me the flowers. "Happy birthday."

I thanked him and closed the door. My mom had called me earlier and said to expect a package from her and my dad today. I wondered if this was what she meant. Deep down, I hoped they were from Jett, but how would he know it was my birthday?

I took them into the kitchen and placed them on the counter. I would put them on the table after we ate.

"Those are pretty," Livy said. "Who are they from?"

"I haven't read the card." I pulled it out and read it. It said, *Happy Birthday to the #1 prettiest plant in Muddy Creek. I know these roses don't compare, but they are a nice second. Love, Jett.*

"Wow, that's bad, but I'll take it," I muttered. I'd been teased about having a plant name before, so this was better. I would give Jett points for trying to be creative.

"What's bad?" Livy asked.

"Nothing," I said, sticking the card in my pocket.

"So?" José asked. "Who are they from?"

Boyd grinned. "Do we even have to ask?"

"When did you start dating Jett?" Livy asked. "I mean, you both watched each other all the time, but you weren't cuddling on the recliner before I left for school."

I knew my face was pink, so I went to the sink to wash my hands. "We aren't dating exactly."

"Hogwash," Boyd said. "They're dating. They'll be married and have two kids by this time next year."

Livy giggled, and José laughed.

"You know it takes nine months to have a baby, right, Boyd?" José said. How are they going to have two in a year?

"Twins?"

I smiled. "You guys are crazy. Jett and I have never even been on a date."

Livy raised her brow. "But you cuddle, and he sends you flowers?"

"And what about all that kissing when we were at the Clementses' house in January?" Boyd asked.

"Jett doesn't have time to date," José said. "You might as well skip it and get married."

I shook my head. "What about the three of you? Should we talk about your love lives?"

"She said love!" Boyd said. "You all heard it. She loves Jett."

"I'm going to talk to Hannah," I said. "You guys can tease each other while I'm gone." I heard them all laughing as I grabbed my coat and left the apartment. Why did I surround myself with people who liked to embarrass me?

I smiled as I walked down the steps. They weren't wrong, though. I was pretty sure I was in love with Jett.

The air wasn't as cold today, and the sky was blue instead of gray. I smiled as I breathed out and didn't see my breath. I was ready to put this frigid Kansas winter behind me. Everyone said this was the worst one in twenty years, and I believed it.

I walked to the B&B and knocked on the door. Miss Medley opened it and frowned. "You know you don't have to knock."

"Oh. Sorry."

"Come in," she said. "What do you want?"

"I'm here to talk to Hannah Taylor."

"She's probably in there," she said, pointing.

"Thanks." I walked in the direction she pointed and came to a large room. It had a few round tables in the middle and ping-pong, foosball, and air hockey tables on the sides. I always thought of B&Bs a little differently, but this room was packed with the corn kids playing games and talking.

Hannah sat at a table, glaring at a glass of water in front of her. I didn't ask if I could sit; I just did.

"Hi, Hannah."

She met my gaze. "Hello."

"How are things?"

She looked around. "Better than being in the snow. As soon as this is all over, I'm going home and never listening to a guy again. I heard Noah is in jail."

I nodded. "He's your boyfriend?"

"Usually."

"Usually?"

"He dumps me about once a month, but he always begs me to take him back. We're perfect together, but he doesn't always see it. Why did he get arrested? No one seems to know."

"I'm not sure the exact charges, but he had a bunch of drugs, and he held people at gunpoint. He also tried to make the sheriff fall asleep so he could break into the sheriff's office to get the drugs back. I wonder if he had something to do with Jacob's death." I watched her carefully.

Hannah's eyes narrowed. "He's not a killer."

"What about all the other stuff?"

She shrugged. "Where do you suppose they put drugs once the police take them?"

"I have no idea. Not at the sheriff's office, though. I bet they were sent to Wichita or something. Did you know Noah was into drugs?"

"He's not. Noah is a health freak. He would never think of harming his body that way."

"So he just sells them?"

She pursed her lips. "Why is Livy out of jail? She's the killer."

"No one thinks she actually did it. They aren't holding her without more evidence."

She rolled her eyes. "So they're letting a killer run loose?"

"I'm sure the sheriff will figure it all out."

"Are you sure they wouldn't keep the drugs at the sheriff's office?"

"I heard the sheriff say they weren't there. Why do you care where they are?"

She took a sip of water. "I'm just curious. Do you think I can see Noah?"

"I don't know."

"This town is boring. I can't wait until this is all over, and I'm sitting on a first-class seat to Cali."

"I bet." I wondered how she was planning on paying for that ticket. Didn't she mention she didn't have any money?

She put her head on the table, and I took that as my cue to leave.

I wandered aimlessly around the town square. With the diner closed, it looked like my apartment was the place for people who didn't know where to go to hang out, and I wasn't in the mood to be teased.

I walked past Jett's office, and he came jogging up to me. "Hey," he said.

"Hello. Thanks for the flowers. How did you know it was my birthday?"

He grinned. "I know many things. Do you want to drive with me to Wichita? I need to take those drugs in."

"Where are you keeping them?"

"In a safe in my office."

"I thought you said they weren't in the office?"

"I lied. Hop in my truck, and I'll be there in a minute. Ledford insisted on coming in today, and I doubt you want to talk to him." He was right. I went over to Jett's big Cybertruck and climbed into the passenger seat. He came back and threw something in the back, then got in and pulled away from the office.

"How's Noah?" I asked.

"Fine. A little crazy, maybe. He's not denying anything."

"Did you ask if he killed Jacob?"

"Yes. He did deny that one."

"Do you think he did it?"

"I'm not sure. He definitely hated Jacob. I've gotten so much done today. Sleep cures so much. I might need to buy myself a recliner just like yours and sleep in that."

I grinned. "Just get a new mattress."

"I might. I've been thinking. It wasn't just the recliner that helped me. Going home to an empty house depresses me. I get home, eat a frozen dinner, and go to bed. Then I'm up at four o'clock to exercise and to do it all again. It was nice to be with friends and wake up to people I care about. I think I need that."

My heart began pounding. "Most people do."

"I think I have a solution."

"Oh?" I tried to act naturally.

"Boyd hates living so far from town. I'm going to ask him if he wants to be my roommate. José too. I know his house is a little run down. He might want to sell."

I crossed my arms and tried not to look disappointed. What did I expect? That he was going to propose? Boyd was giving me weird thoughts in my head.

"Do you think they would?" he asked.

"Maybe. What if they sold their houses, and then it didn't work out? They wouldn't have anywhere to live."

He rubbed his chin. "Why wouldn't it work out?"

"Who knows? And what if you didn't want to live with them forever?"

"I haven't thought that far. It would be nice to get off work and go home and shoot hoops with José or watch a lame movie with Boyd."

I wanted to slink back home and curl up in my bed. If he was making long-term plans like this, where did it leave me?

"Is something wrong?" he asked.

I forced a smile. "No."

"You think it's a terrible idea?"

"Not if it makes you happy. I have to tell you, though. I'm out on a walk because Boyd and José have taken over my place, and they're beginning to drive me crazy."

"I'm not home most of the time, so I don't think they would bother me."

"Boyd is messy. When I saw your house, it was pretty clean."

"With just me, it's not hard to stay clean. I only mop my floors twice a year, and they aren't even dirty then."

If Jett wanted roommates, I would be supportive.

"This truck is awesome. You can connect to the sound system with Bluetooth headphones," Jett said. "I bought some nice ones, and it feels like you're right there with the singer. You should try it." He handed me some headphones, and I put them on. I'm not much of a headphones person, but I would let Jett show off his toys. "Listen to this song while I call Boyd. I want to know if he might be interested in my plan."

I frowned as twangy country music screamed in my ear. I might live in the country, but the country music hasn't grown on me yet. I turned it down.

Jett hooked the earpiece to his phone over his ear. "Hey, Boyd. Is José with you? Can you go on speakerphone? I have a question."

I turned the music down more so I could eavesdrop.

"I'm thinking of taking on some roommates. Are you interested? It would put you close to town." He paused for a moment. "Yep. Mm-hmm—exactly."

I wished I could hear Boyd and José.

"That's what I was thinking," he said. There was a really long pause, then he laughed. "I thought you might say that. I don't see it as a problem. If that happens, you can buy the house from me."

I raised my brows and looked out the window so he wouldn't know I was eavesdropping.

"Yep. No. Well, her apartment is nicer than my house, anyway."

I was having trouble breathing normally. I would pay to hear the other side of the conversation.

"What are you talking about?" he asked. "We go on dates all the time—Yes, we do. Well, I can't go on regular dates. I'm always on duty. We're going to Wichita right now to deliver the drugs." He laughed. "I know. That sounded bad." He was quiet for a full minute. "Okay. Thanks, José. Bye."

I kept staring out the window, wondering if he really thought I hadn't heard that entire conversation. I guess I wouldn't have if I'd left the sound blaring.

He poked me, and I took off the headphones. "Good sound, huh?"

I smiled. "Unless you hate country music."

"Whhhhat? Don't tell me you hate country music."

"I won't. But I do. Are José and Boyd up for it?"

"They're both going to think about it. Boyd sounded optimistic about it. José has a few reservations."

We drove in silence for longer than was comfortable. Jett's jaw was tense, and his forehead was furrowed. I could tell he was thinking, and I didn't want to interrupt him. We drove into Wichita and stopped at the Drug Enforcement Administration. Jett grabbed the bag from behind him.

"I'm not sure how long this will take. Are you okay in here? I'll leave the heat on."

"I'm fine." I leaned against the seat and tried to think over the case. Noah seemed like the logical one to have killed Jacob. He'd had the most to gain. I was wondering about Hannah. She definitely had some issues. I couldn't completely rule out Livy, but I seriously doubted it was her.

Twenty minutes passed before Jett returned. He climbed in and turned to me. "Could Hannah be the one who killed Jacob?"

"That's funny. I was just thinking the same thing. It's possible."

"Let's think about that some more. My bet is on her or Noah."

"Not Carlos?"

"Who is Carlos?"

I laughed. "One of the corn kids. I don't think it was him, but you never know."

"It could have been any of them. Ledford interviewed all of them. I need to go read his notes again. I should probably talk to him as well. Ledford didn't say anything nasty about you today. Maybe he'll tolerate you now that you saved him."

I laughed. "That would be something. I love it when people tolerate me."

He grinned. "Ledford might not be so bad if he didn't feel like he had so much to prove. That's probably my fault. I let you help too much, and it makes him feel challenged."

"You usually tell me to leave it to you. Just in a nicer way than Ledford."

"Yeah, but I don't try as hard anymore. I've realized it's a waste of breath. You're going to do it anyway. I'd rather know what you're doing than have you sneaking around. That reminds me. Do you think you could share your location with me?"

I frowned. "What do you mean?"

"On your phone. Then I can track you. It would make me feel better."

I grinned. "You want to stalk me?"

He rolled his eyes. "No, but it would be nice to be able to track you if anything happened. I'll let you track me too, if it makes you feel better. I'll have to turn it off occasionally for security reasons."

"Deal." I grabbed my phone and messed with the settings until I figured it out.

He pulled up to a drive-through and got us hot chocolate. I love hot chocolate, but I couldn't wait until it was too warm for it.

Chapter 13

Jett took a wrong turn when we got to Muddy Creek, and we ended up on a narrow dirt road. Puddles of mud splattered the truck, so we had to go slowly.

"I thought you knew this place inside out?" I said as we bumped up and down. This road hadn't seen any maintenance in a while.

"Most of it."

"Why don't you turn around?"

"The road is too narrow."

"I'm sure it's okay to drive over the road a little. Who's going to give you a ticket?"

He grinned. "Ledford would love to."

"But he isn't here. Is it really illegal to do a turn?"

"No, but if I keep going, this road eventually goes back to town."

"But won't that take longer?"

"Yep."

I gave up. Jett pointed out a few farms and told me who lived on them. It took a while, but we were finally going back in the direction of town.

"Your truck is going to be so dirty."

"Yeah, but it's a good sign spring is around the corner."

"I've never been so happy for spring."

We drove into town, and Jett passed the diner. There wasn't any parking.

"I wonder why the spaces are filled," I said. "There must be a sale going on at the shop next door. You can just drop me off, and I'll walk."

"No, I'll walk you up to your door." He drove past a few more shops, then turned and went behind them.

"I thought you didn't like people driving back here?"

He shrugged. "We have to park somewhere." He parked in the dirt next to the diner dumpster. "They should put a small road back here. I'm sure the garbage collector would appreciate it."

I stepped out into the mud. I couldn't believe how fast the snow was melting in the areas that had been shoveled.

"I wonder if José and Boyd are still here," I said. "I might have to kick them out, eventually."

"They were when I called." We walked up the stairs, and I felt my stomach flutter. Why was he walking me to the door? Was I supposed to stand at the door awkwardly and hope he kissed me? No. He was on duty. He'd only ever kissed me when he wasn't.

I pulled open the door and turned to say goodbye. He grinned and grabbed my arms, turning me around. He pushed me gently into the front room.

"Happy Birthday!" a chorus of voices yelled. My eyes were wide as I stared at the room full of people. The area was packed.

I put my hand to my heart. "Oh my goodness! You all nearly gave me a heart attack!"

Barbra laughed. "You're too young for that. Now get in here and close the door. It's still cold out."

Jett closed the door, and I turned to him. "Is this why we got lost on the way home?"

He grinned. "Possibly."

José walked from the kitchen carrying a white cake with purple flowers. Everyone started singing. I'd never had this many people staring at me while singing, and I wished I had run a brush through my hair. I felt goofy, but I put on a smile.

"Thank you all," I said when the song ended. I blew out a single gold candle, and everyone clapped.

"I'll take the cake back to the kitchen, and Livy and I will serve you," José said. "Ivy can open her presents while we get it to everyone."

"Sit in the recliner," Boyd said. I sank into the chair, realizing everyone would be staring at me a bit longer.

"Who planned this?" I asked.

Boyd scratched his head. "Well, Jett had the idea. He told José and me, and we got Barbra and Opal involved. Then Barbra and Opal took over."

"I didn't get much say," Opal said. "If I had, there never would have been a cake with that much frosting. José overdid it for sure."

I smiled. "Well, thank you."

Boyd handed me a present wrapped in newspaper. I found that funny since I knew he had a ton of money. You would never know it to look at him. I unwrapped it and found a purple pocket knife.

"Look at the blade," Boyd said. I flipped it open. It had my name on it.

"Thanks, Boyd."

"Yep. Now, if you see someone tied up, you have something to use. Just don't drop it when you're sneaking around, or people will know you were there."

"How often do you think she'll find someone tied up?" Opal asked.

I gave a half smile. "It happens more than you might think."

"I got you this," Anton said, handing me a bag. I pulled out a headlamp. That would have come in handy a few times. Now, I just needed a tool belt to carry everything so I would always be prepared. I pictured myself wearing a tool belt and smiled.

Jett grabbed something from behind my chair. He held up the hideous neon cat apron he had given me when I first took over the diner. "Here's my present," he said. He held the apron up and ripped it.

I covered my mouth. The apron was hideous, but I loved it because he gave it to me. A few people cheered.

Jett grabbed a purple gift bag and handed it to me. I pulled out the tissue paper and then a lavender apron. I smiled. It was beautiful. Much better than neon. "Thank you. I don't think I can wear it. I don't want to get it dirty."

"Go ahead and get it dirty. I got you a spare. It's hanging downstairs in the diner."

I felt my eyes starting to tear. Barbra tossed a present on my lap. I opened it to find a stuffed teddy bear holding a box of chocolates. The bear had a purple necktie. I'd never told anyone here my favorite color was purple, but they seemed to know. I opened the rest of the presents while people ate cake.

Everyone was talking and having a good time. I smiled. I'd never had a surprise party before. It had been awkward, but it was nice to know I had people here who cared about me.

Jett's watch beeped. "I have one more present," he said, pulling me to my feet. He was holding a shoebox. "Can we go someplace where we can be alone for a few minutes?"

"Is that allowed?" Boyd asked.

"Of course it's allowed," Barbra said. "But we will hold you to the few minutes."

"Ten?" Jett asked.

"Hmm. Alright."

Jett kept my hand and took me into my room, then shut the door. He handed me the shoebox.

"You got me size 12 men's running shoes?"

He laughed. "No."

I took off the lid. It was full of bite-sized Caramellos. I smiled. "These are my favorite."

"I remembered something about that." He sat on my window seat, and I sat on the end of my bed. Creepers meowed and climbed up to my pillow.

Jett took a deep breath. "Do you think we can have the talk?"

I tilted my head. "It depends on what the talk is."

"You know. The talk where we define our relationship?"

I swallowed, and my heart started wreaking havoc on the rest of my insides. "Umm, okay."

"I was talking to Boyd today, and he said that you said we've never been on a date."

I shrugged. "We haven't."

"So I've pretty much thought we were close to dating since you moved here. I've counted us as dating in my head since we were at the Clementses' in January."

I took a deep breath.

He raked a hand through his hair. "I know that makes me crazy. I can't date while I'm on duty, but I've counted every time we're together as cheat dates. Sure, going to the cemetery or disposing of drugs isn't romantic or anything, but I don't get a lot of downtime. There aren't a lot of places to go in this town. I could take you to the diner, but you own it."

I smiled. "I don't mind the cemetery."

"I guess what I'm saying is, I want to know what you think about us. Where do you see us ending up?"

I rubbed my lips together. "Can't you answer that first?"

Leaning forward, he rested his elbows on his legs and stared into my eyes. "I see you, me, three kids, and a dog."

I blinked. He couldn't be more straightforward than that. "How about four kids and no dog?"

He grinned. "Four kids, and we're into minivan territory."

"Are you scared of minivans?"

"A little. Are you scared of dogs?"

"I haven't been around them much. I thought you were trying to phase me out."

He frowned. "What do you mean?"

"You've barely answered my texts since we were at the Clementses', and you haven't talked to me much."

"I'm sorry. I've been so busy and so tired, and I worry about being around you when I'm on duty. I hate it when Ledford's right, but I do have to be careful of my image.

When I'm with you, I don't feel like being professional. I need to be careful about what I'm doing when I'm on duty."

I stood. "But not on call?"

"Not as much. I'm always on call if I'm not on duty."

Someone banged on the door, and Boyd poked his head in. "Barbra said it's been ten minutes."

Jett stood. "Tell her to give us three more. Make that five."

Boyd looked over his shoulder. "He wants five more minutes." I couldn't understand Barbra's answer, but Boyd shut the door.

Jett turned and put his arms around my waist, then smiled. "I didn't shave for three days in preparation for your birthday."

I groaned and put my arms around his neck. "I can't believe Boyd told you that."

"You like scruff, and I don't like to shave. It's perfect."

I ran my hand over his prickly cheek. "We only have five minutes. Are you going to kiss me or what?"

Chapter 14

"Good job today, ladies!" I turned off the music in the dance studio and grabbed my water bottle. Jett was going to talk to the mayor today and see if we could open the diner. He thought he could convince him, but I wasn't sure. Mayor Jepson didn't seem reasonable to me.

"I'm getting better at this Zumba stuff," Opal said. "I can even bend down and pick things up since I've been doing it."

"I told you," Barbra said. "Ivy's going easy on us, though. She doesn't want us all ending up in the hospital because we twisted too hard." It was true. I'd changed all the moves to fit our needs.

"Where is Boyd today?" someone asked.

Barbra laughed. "He partied too hard last night."

"I never thought of him as a party person."

"He's not. I was joking. He has stitches and has to rest until they come out. He ate three pieces of cake last night, though."

Boyd really could take down the cake. I'd had half a piece, and that was all I could take. Of course, I'd been distracted since I'd just spent five minutes kissing Jett.

"I'll see you all next week." I tossed my gym bag over my shoulder and locked the studio. Avoiding mud puddles was hard, but I would take all the mud puddles if it meant not having it snow. It would take a while for all the piles of snow to melt. When I got to the diner, I paused. A shadow crossed the window. No one should be down there. Livy wouldn't come down, and Boyd was having trouble with stairs.

I texted Livy to ask if she was down there. She texted back that she was going for a short walk with Boyd and was just around the corner. I told her not to come back until I told her. I called Jett. He wouldn't be happy if I went in without him.

"Hey, Ivs. Miss me?"

"Yep, but that's not why I'm calling. I just got home, and someone is in the diner. It's not Livy or Boyd."

"Don't go down."

"I'm still outside."

"Stay there. I'm coming."

I moved to the side of the diner so no one would see me if they peeked out the window. I watched down the road and waited. Waiting isn't my strong point. I looked up and saw a shadow on my bedroom window. My mouth turned down. Creepers was up there. I was giving Jett one minute, then I was going in.

Jett's truck came around the corner, and I headed toward it. He parked and got out.

"I saw them in my bedroom window."

"You're sure it's not José or something?" he asked.

"Why would José be in my room? They were in the diner then went up—or there might be more than one person."

"I'll go; you stay here."

I frowned but nodded. That would allow me to watch and make sure they didn't escape. I handed Jett the key, and he turned it quietly in the lock. Being in the back of the building might be better. If Jett went up the stairs, they were more likely to escape out the back. Just as I got to the back, a person in black with a mask ran out my door and began tearing down the stairs. I ran toward them, and they jumped over the rail and landed clumsily but got back up and ran.

"Jett!" I yelled. I wasn't sure he heard me, so I rushed after the person. From the build of the person, I guessed it was a woman. She headed straight back from the diner, which would take her to the middle of nowhere. There was nothing that way except flat land, as far as could be seen. That made me think it was someone not native to the area.

Glass breaking made me flip around and frown. Someone had just broken the glass from my living room window. That was new! I debated going after the woman or
helping Jett. The woman was still running. If she kept
going, she would be easy to find since there was nowhere
to go.

I hurried back toward my home when another figure
dressed in black came running from my place. He jumped
down the last five steps, then turned left and ran. I focused
and ran at him. When he turned and saw me, he tripped
and fell flat in the snow. Jett came running from the apartment, and I jumped on the man so he wouldn't get away.

He tried to throw me off so he could get up, but I had
a good grip on him. His head came back and hit me in the
eye, but it wasn't hard enough to shake me. He'd probably
done it by accident.

"Get off, Ivs," Jett said, running up. I rolled off, and Jett
grabbed and pulled the guy to his feet. The guy tried to
punch Jett, but Jett ducked, then slammed him into a tree
and cuffed his hands. He ripped off the mask, and Carlos
looked guiltily up at him.

"Carlos?" I said. "I didn't expect this."

Carlos frowned. "It's not my fault. It wasn't my idea."

"What wasn't?" Jett asked.

"Breaking in."

"It doesn't matter whose idea it was."

"Someone got by me," I said. She's running over there."
I pointed at the person getting smaller in the distance.

Jett rolled his eyes. "Where does she think she's going? It'll take days to come to the nearest city that way."

"Who is that?" I asked.

Carlos shrugged. "Just someone passing through."

Jett pulled him forward. "You decided to break into a business with a random person just passing through?"

"I'll go after her," I said.

Jett looked over his shoulder. "No. After I lock him up, I'll grab the four-wheeler and go after her."

"You have a four-wheeler?"

"It belongs to the county. You never know what you might need around here."

"I can watch them and see if they come back around. They're going to have to realize they aren't going to get anywhere going straight."

"Alright, but don't go after them. Text Ledford, tell him what happened, and tell him to get the four-wheeler ready."

I pulled out my phone, and Jett gave me Ledford's number before he hurried away with Carlos.

I texted Ledford, then sat on the stairs and watched the person get farther and farther away. Jett really needed more manpower. There were never enough people around here to get things done.

Sometime later, a vehicle came into view. It came from town and was moving toward the person. Jett was sure taking his time unless that was him on the four-wheeler. I felt like I'd been waiting forever. The vehicle got to the person and stopped. They must have picked up the mysterious figure because when it started again, all I could see was the vehicle.

Jett came running around the corner. "Someone stole the four-wheeler."

"Did it look like that?" I asked, pointing in the distance.

Jett squinted. "It might be. If they keep going, they'll hit the road before we can get to them."

"I bet it was Hannah."

"Yeah?"

"There's something off when I talk to her. I should have kept running after her, but I freaked out when the window broke."

"I was chasing the girl, and I didn't realize Carlos was in there. He tripped me, and she got out. When I got up, he threw something at me, and it went through the window. What happened to your eye?"

"Carlos head-butted me. I think it was an accident. It doesn't hurt that much."

"It's going to bruise."

I shrugged. I'd had a few weird bruises since coming to Muddy Creek.

"I'll go after them, then I'll run over to the B&B and see if Hannah's there," he said.

"I'll tell Boyd and Livy they can come back."

Jett left, and I texted Boyd, then went inside to inspect the damage. It looked like the only problem was the window.

Boyd and Livy came in, and Boyd sat on the couch. He leaned back and sighed. "I think I overdid it. Did you catch anyone? What happened to the window?"

"Carlos and someone else were here. We got Carlos, but not the other one."

Livy frowned. "Carlos? I never would have suspected him. I bet someone bullied him into it."

"At least one more person is helping. They stole the police four-wheeler and picked up the other person we lost."

"Noah's family has a lot of money. It's possible he's promised people things," Livy said.

"But why break in here?" I asked. "You two should check your things and make sure none of it was disturbed."

Livy went into her room, and Boyd just yawned. "I don't have anything important here."

"You probably shouldn't go walking around until your knee heals."

"Those stairs are killer on the knees on a good day. The walking isn't as bad. Where's Jett?"

"He's going to see if he can find the people on the four-wheeler, then he'll go to the B&B to see who was missing. It's too bad Ledford can't help."

I'd failed. I should have driven over and at least tried to see who they were or volunteered to go to the B&B. The roads over where the four-wheeler should be were unfamiliar to me, and it probably would have been a waste of time. That was what I would tell myself. Still, going to the B&B would have been easy.

Livy came into the room wringing her hands. "Ivy? Come see this."

I followed her to her room. Her duffel bag was on the bed, and she pulled it open and pointed inside. There was something sitting on top. It was long with an orange cap and almost looked like a fat pen.

"What is it?" I asked.

"It's an EpiPen. I bet whoever broke in put it there, and I bet it's Jacob's. The one that someone replaced with a fake. They're trying to frame me even more."

I put my hand on her arm. "Don't worry about that. Jett and Ledford both searched your things. They would have found it, so they'd know someone had planted it. Just don't touch it and get prints on it."

"I don't understand why someone would frame me."

"What happened when you found Jacob's EpiPen? The fake one?"

"It was in the snow, so I grabbed it and took it to him."

"Was anyone with you?"

"Yeah, Hannah pointed it out to me. She had her hands in her pockets, so I picked it up and took it to him."

"I bet Hannah threw it there and then pointed it out to you."

Livy's mouth turned down. "Maybe. Hannah's not big on ideas. I wouldn't think she could pull anything off."

"Maybe Carlos helped plan it."

"I still think he's just getting bossed by her. They never talked much or anything."

"But what if they did that so no one would suspect?"

"I guess so. I just hope we figure it out before I have to go to jail again."

There was a pounding on the front door, so I went out to get it before Boyd stood and hurt himself again. I opened the door, and Jett came in.

"Did you find them?" I asked.

"No. I went to the B&B, and Hannah wasn't there, but neither were five of the corn kids."

"Do you think all five of them are working together?"

"I have no idea. One of the kids who was still there said they all went on a walk. I drove around and didn't see any of them. I know Ledford has a concussion, but I might need to find him and see if he can help."

"Isn't he at your office?"

"No, he wasn't there."

I pulled my phone out. I had a text from him. "He texted me when I told him to get the four-wheeler ready. He said, got it."

Jett pulled out his phone, then pushed a few buttons and put it to his ear. "He's not answering."

"Could he have been the person on the four-wheeler?" I asked.

"Did you tell him where you were?"

"Yeah, I told them I was watching from the back of the diner."

"That could be good. Maybe he brought her in. I'm going to run over to the office. I'll see you soon."

I watched him rush away and sighed. I needed to go shower, and then I would go see if Ledford had caught anyone. The diner needed to open soon. If it didn't, I would go crazy.

Chapter 15

Mayor Jepson stood at my door in his suit, staring at his watch. "I've been standing out here pounding on the door for five minutes. My time is important."

My hair was dripping from my shower. I'd heard him pounding on the door and hurried to get out and answer. "What do you need?"

"I'm going to let you reopen the diner starting tomorrow."

I nodded. "Thanks."

"And I want to reserve the party room for Saturday."

It figured. He was only letting me open because he wanted something. "Alright. What time?"

"Seven."

"Okay, thanks."

"Try to keep any of those college kids from the diner that day. I don't know why the sheriff isn't throwing them all out of town."

"He has to find out what happened first."

"It's taking too long. The sheriff seems overly distracted these days." He gave me a knowing glance, and I frowned. I wanted to argue with him, but I also wanted the diner to stay open. It was getting warmer, and we might begin to get more customers again.

I called José to let him know we would be open the next day. He might have been more excited than me. Making José the manager had taken a lot of stress from me. He was good at organizing things, and everyone liked him.

I grabbed a jacket and headed for the sheriff's office. Jane told me to go into Jett's office. I knocked on the door, then went in. Jett sat at a large desk, typing something into the computer.

"Hey, Ivs," he said. "It was Ledford on the four-wheeler."

"Did he catch someone?"

"He did, but when he got into town, he was feeling dizzy, and they were able to run off."

"And he didn't take their mask off?"

"No. I sent him home and told him not to come back until he has a note from his doctor saying he's able to work."

"That's a good idea."

"I've gotten some good news."

"Oh?"

"Now that we've had so much crime, it's grabbed some people's attention. The budget was re-evaluated, and they posted a few job offerings to get more officers here. They're offering more money, and it looks like there have been a few applicants. They're also hiring more people to help in the office."

"That's great."

"Yep. I might get to take normal shifts soon."

"Did you get Carlos to tell you anything?"

"No. I think he might eventually."

"I'm going to see if Hannah's back at the B&B."

Jett frowned. "Be careful and stay around people."

On my way to the B&B, I saw Hannah walking down the sidewalk with two other young women. They were talking and laughing. When Hannah saw me, she waved, so I hurried across the street to talk.

"Hi," I said. "What are you three up to?"

"We just went to a movie," Hannah said. "It was pretty lame, but the theater here only has one option."

"There's a theater?" I asked. I'd never seen one.

Hannah shrugged. "It's kinda pathetic. It's two buildings away from the library." I remembered a building that looked like it had been a theater, but I'd thought it was out of business. "It only plays one movie, and it's only open for one showing a day."

"And you were all there?"

"Yes."

"The entire time?"

One of the girls laughed. "Why wouldn't we be? It wouldn't make sense to leave during part of it."

"Where are the rest of your friends?"

"I'm not sure we're all friends anymore," Hannah said. "Carlos and Patrice went somewhere together today."

"They're a horrible couple," one girl said.

"Agreed," said Hannah. "Carlos is pretty open and friendly, and Patrice is always trying to be mysterious."

"Mysterious, how?" I was trying to remember who Patrice was. I thought she might be one of the girls leaping around throwing flowers when we'd gone to the camp.

"She's fairly quiet, but she's always where she shouldn't be. I'm almost positive she stole my shampoo."

"And you're sure she was with Carlos today?"

"Yeah. They left before we went to the movie."

"Are you headed back to the B&B? I'd like to see if she's there."

"No, we don't like to hang around there."

"There aren't a lot of places to go around here."

"Yeah, we wish the diner was open."

"It will be tomorrow."

Hannah grinned. "Oh, good. We'll be there." I wondered how she was going to pay. "If you go looking for

Patrice, you might find her sitting in the corner of the common room with a book."

"Thanks." I left the group and hurried to Miss Medley's place. Hannah didn't look like someone who had been breaking into places, running around in the cold, and escaping from Ledford. Her hair was neat, and she didn't look nervous.

I went into the B&B and to the common room. Two boys were playing pool, and a girl with short brown hair was sitting in an overstuffed chair in the corner, reading.

I made my way over to her. She glanced up at me, then back down at her book.

"Hi," I said. "I don't know if you remember me. I'm Ivy."

She didn't look up. "I remember."

"Can I ask you a few questions?"

She pushed some hair behind her ear and sighed. "I don't know anything. The sheriff and that other guy keep coming and asking us things, and I don't know about Jacob, Noah, or anything."

"So you know where Carlos is?"

"I think he went on a walk or something."

"He's in jail."

That made her look up. "Oh? That's too bad."

"He broke into my diner earlier today."

She closed her book and put it on her lap. "Wow."

"Do you know who he was with today?"

"No."

"You weren't with him?"

She pursed her lips and stared at me. "Why would I be with him?"

"I don't know. Someone said you were."

"I've never done anything with him. He doesn't even believe in astrological signs. He makes fun of them."

My brows came together. "Okay. So you haven't talked to him today?"

"Not that I remember. Can I go back to my book, please?"

I nodded. I couldn't read Patrice. She was already back to reading her book and ignoring me. I left the building and stared down the street. I felt like I was wasting time, and I didn't know what to do with myself. My phone rang, taking me away from my thoughts.

"Hello?"

"It's Jett. Can you do me a favor?"

"Sure."

"Would you go to my house and into my office and get a manila folder off the desk?"

"I can do that." I started walking in the direction of his house. "Is the house locked?"

"Yeah, but I keep a key under the mat."

I laughed. "And you call yourself a lawman? That's the first place anyone is going to look."

"I know. I'm lazy and can't think of a better place."

"You're the least lazy person I know. Hey, I saw Hannah. She just got out of a movie. She had two friends with her, so if she was the one at my place, her friends are lying for her. I also talked to a girl named Patrice. Hannah said she was with Carlos today."

"Interesting. I've talked to her a few times. She never was on my radar, but maybe she should be."

"I'll grab your folder and bring it to you soon."

"Thanks, Ivs. I appreciate you, and I'm not just saying that."

I hung up and walked slowly to his house. He hadn't said to hurry, and I was tired. When I got there, I lifted the mat and found the key. I opened the door and went in. I'd only been here once, and I had no idea where his office was. Wandering around Jett's house made me feel funny, but he'd asked me to come here.

I couldn't see anything that looked like an office, so I went upstairs. The office was the first room after the stairs. I went in and grabbed the folder from the desk, and paused when I heard the door shut downstairs. Could Jett have come back? I pulled my phone out to check his location. It said he was still at the sheriff's office.

Someone was walking around, and they weren't trying to be quiet. I scrolled to Jett's number on my phone and pushed it.

"Did you find it?" Jett asked.

"Yes. Are you expecting someone?"

"No."

"I'm in your office, but there's someone downstairs."

"On my way." He hung up. I felt like I'd been in this situation more than was natural. Jett was probably thinking the same thing.

Looking around the room, I spotted a trophy. I didn't take the time to examine it. I just grabbed it and walked carefully across the floor, hoping it wouldn't creak. I walked softly down the stairs. Something in me wanted to run for the front door, but a stronger part of me wanted to see who was here. Whoever it was couldn't be here for legitimate reasons.

The toilet flushed, so I walked quietly toward the bathroom. The door was closed. I stood there holding the trophy like a baseball bat. The door slowly opened, and Carol Malone stood there holding a toilet scrubber and wearing long rubber gloves. Her eyes widened when she saw me. My arm lowered, and I covered my pounding heart.

"Ivy?" she said. "What are you doing here?"

"Jett asked me to grab something. Are you cleaning his bathroom?"

She grinned. "I know. He's thirty-three. He should clean his own bathroom. I'm Jett's mom, so I can tell when he's struggling and that boy is struggling. I know he doesn't have a lot of time, so once a week, I come in and clean his bathrooms and mop everything."

"Does he know?"

"No, but he really should keep his key hidden some-where more secure."

I giggled. "He thinks his house just automatically stays clean. He told me he only mops twice a year."

Carol laughed. "You would think he would be able to smell the cleaning products."

The front door burst open, and Jett came running in, holding his gun. He looked down the hall, and his mouth turned down. "Mom? What are you doing here?" He walked over, sounding suspicious.

"Cleaning your toilet."

He put his gun away. "Why?"

She looked at me and winked. "Because you never know who might come over and see your mess and get scared away."

"Do you do this often?"

"Once a week, when the weather is good."

"Is that my trophy?" he asked me.

"I thought I might need a weapon."

I handed him the folder. "Sorry I called you. I know you're busy. I should have checked down here first."

"No," he said, running his hand over my cheek. "Always call. It's better to be safe." He kissed me quickly, and I decided not to remind him he was on duty. "I do have to get back, though."

"I'll go put this away," I said, holding up the trophy.

"Thanks." He kissed me again and hurried out the door. I stared at the closed door, smiling.

"That was interesting," Carol said. I jumped. How had I forgotten she was there?

"I better take this up," I said, rushing toward the stairs. I put the trophy back where I found it and went back down.

Carol had taken off the gloves and put away the toilet cleaner. She crossed her arms but smiled. "So what's going on with you and my son?"

"We're working on a case."

"You know that's not what I mean. I've been waiting years for that boy to find someone special, and I want all the details."

The door opened again, and Jett poked his head in. "Come on, Ivs, you better leave. I just realized I left you here with my mom, and she's going to get all nosy." He came over, grabbed my hand, and pulled me toward the door.

Carol grinned. "You better believe I am. You can't kiss a girl in front of me and run away without giving me the story."

"I'm really busy, Ma."

"Fine, but just tell me how serious this thing is."

Jett grinned. "Don't you listen to the town gossip?"

Carol pushed a brown curl behind her ear. "You know it's hard for me to get into town. Are you official?"

Jett put his arm over my shoulders. "We're official."

"And you didn't tell your mom?"

"I just did."

"But I had to pull it out of you."

"It only technically became official yesterday. I haven't had time to breathe, or I would have come and told you."

She smiled. "Alright, I'll forgive you this time. If you decide to run off and elope, you will regret it, though. You're my only baby, and I need to be there for that."

I smiled at the thought of Jett being called a baby.

Jett chuckled. "Got it. No eloping."

Chapter 16

When José walked into the diner the next day, he stopped and tilted his head when he saw me. I smiled. I never beat him to the diner in the morning even though I lived above it. My whisk was in one hand, and I held a bowl tightly against me in the other.

"What are you doing?" he asked.

"Making pancakes."

He groaned. "I mean this in a nice way, Ivy. Leave the meals to me."

"I know I'm usually only good at dessert, but I saw this recipe online last night and really want to try it. It looks more like a dessert than actual pancakes."

He came and peeked into the bowl. "It's too thick."

"I followed the recipe."

"They won't cook well. The outside will burn before the inside cooks."

I grinned. "We'll see."

José raised his eyebrow. "Yes, we will."

Jett was talking to all the college students again today, and he had begged me to stay here while he did it. I needed to do something to keep myself distracted. The skillet was warm, so I sprayed it with cooking spray and poured the batter on.

"It's too hot," José said. "It's going to burn."

I narrowed my eyes. "Don't you have anything to do?"

He laughed. "Plenty. I'm just trying to save you some ingredients." He went to the fridge and rummaged around.

I'd put a post on the town's social media page, letting people know the diner was open again. The sun was out today, and there wasn't any wind, so I hoped we would have a good turnout.

I flipped my test pancake and smiled. It looked perfect. José would even have to agree.

Anton came in and pulled an apron over his head. "It's good to be back. My life is so boring. I've missed work."

"Livy's coming to help," José said. "I texted her because all our servers are a bit skittish about coming in until everything is solved."

I frowned. "Is that a good idea?"

"Innocent until proven guilty. If people have a problem with that, they can eat somewhere else."

I nodded. "It will probably be good for her. I think she's going crazy sitting in my apartment all day with Boyd and Creepers."

"Won't Boyd be bored by himself?" Anton asked.

"Maybe, but he seems pretty good at entertaining himself. Creepers loves having him there. He spoils that cat."

"Is Carrie coming?" I asked.

"No. I told her we'd call if we needed her, but I thought we should wait and see how busy we are first."

I grabbed the plastic spatula and put the pancake on a plate. It was beautiful. I smiled and handed it to José. He shook his head and placed it on the island, and grabbed a fork. He cut a piece, and batter oozed out.

"What?" I exclaimed. "It looked amazing!"

He grinned. "Your batter is too thick, and your skillet is too hot."

I wrinkled my nose. "I hate it when you're right."

He laughed. "But it's why you keep me working here. Let me see your recipe." I handed him the paper I'd printed out.

Livy came in and smiled. "I'm excited to work again. I've missed this place." She'd left her hair down and curled it. She usually wore it in a ponytail.

"You look nice," Anton said.

Livy blushed and smiled. "Thanks."

Anton looked stressed for a moment, like he didn't know how to continue the conversation, then he went and turned on the oven.

José was doing something to the pancake batter. I should probably watch and see what, but I was watching Anton and Livy.

"We're open in ten, people," José said. "And there are already customers standing outside."

I looked through the window and smiled. I could see someone standing by the doors. Muddy Creek was a great town, and I was sure they were coming to show support.

"Should we let them in?" I asked. I didn't want to lose any customers because they had to stand outside too long.

"Sure," José said. "Livy, will you open the doors?"

She nodded and hurried out. She opened the doors, and I watched three groups of people come in and sit.

"We might need to call Carrie," I said.

José looked out. "Maybe, but I bet we can handle it. As long as Anton focuses on cooking and not Livy."

Anton's head whipped around, and he glared at José. "You're crazy. Livy's just a friend."

"Yes, but by choice, or because you're too scared to make a move?"

I smiled, glad José's teasing wasn't aimed at me.

Anton ignored José.

Livy rushed in and grabbed some glasses and began filling them with water. "I need two hot chocolates."

"I'm on it," Anton said. She grabbed an ordering pad and disappeared with the water.

"Patrice is out there," I said, glancing out into the diner. The girl was sitting by herself, staring out the front window. I wished I knew what to do. If Patrice was the one who had broken in yesterday, then I needed to watch her. I didn't think she was the one who killed Jacob. She hadn't been at the diner when it happened, so she wouldn't have been able to put the syrup dispenser on the table. But she might be an accomplice if she'd been working with someone.

We knew Carlos had broken in yesterday. He was also at the diner the day Jacob died. The two of them could have been working together that day as well. It made the most sense of anything I'd come up with, but I still had a nagging feeling about Hannah.

The morning flew by. I spent it baking desserts because dinner was the time most people ordered them. Patrice hadn't left. She sat in her booth reading a book and drinking hot chocolate. She's had three mugs of it and didn't look like she had any plans to leave. When lunch rolled around, Patrice stood and hugged the book to herself and walked slowly through the diner. She watched me as she went out the door.

I pulled my apron and hairnet off. "José, I'll be back."

"Where are you going?" he asked from where he was frying something.

"I'm following Patrice."

I hurried through the dining area and out the front door. Patrice was walking briskly down the walkway. I strolled behind her, trying not to draw her attention. She turned and walked across the street. She never looked back, so I kept following her.

When she got to the library, she went in. I'd followed her for no reason. She was only returning her book. I went inside and watched her drop her book in the return bin and walk over to the young adult section.

Brian looked up from his desk and smiled. "Hi, Ivy. Is there anything I can help you with?"

I walked over to his desk and leaned near him. "Do you know Patrice?" I asked quietly.

He looked over to where the girl had gone. "She comes in a lot. She reads about one book a day." He tilted his head. "I know that look. Do you think she did something?"

"Two people broke into my place yesterday morning while I was teaching Zumba. One of them was caught, but not the other. Someone told us Patrice was with the guy we caught."

Brian shook his head. "Patrice was here yesterday morning. She was sitting in the corner of the library reading."

"And she didn't look like she'd been out running through the snow or anything?"

"Nope."

I sighed. Patrice walked to the end of the shelf and looked at me. She smiled slightly and walked down another aisle. She was up to something, but I couldn't understand what.

A siren sounded outside. "That doesn't sound like Jett's siren, does it?" I asked.

"No, that's the fire truck."

"I wonder what's going on."

Brian walked over to the door and poked his head out. He came back. "I see smoke down the road. I can't tell what it is."

"I should go check."

Patrice came over, holding a book. "You should stay here. Fires can be dangerous."

I cocked my head and looked at her. "What are you doing? What's your game?"

Patrice frowned. "What do you mean?"

"You wanted me to follow you here, and now you don't want me to leave. Who are you helping and why?"

Patrice's mouth turned down, and her grip on the book tightened. "I haven't done anything."

"The things going on here have been serious. Do you really want to end up in jail?"

Her lip quivered slightly. "Why would I go to jail?"

"For helping people do illegal things."

"I'm not doing anything illegal."

"You are if you're helping someone who is hiding something."

She tossed the book onto Brian's desk. "Sometimes things can't be helped."

"But they usually can. Make the right decision, or you'll end up in trouble."

She folded her arms and rubbed them. "I'm supposed to distract you. I don't know why."

My eyes narrowed. "For who? Hannah?"

She nodded. "I don't know anything. I just do what she says because she threatens me."

"Jett's going to be at the fire," Brian said. "Is that a distraction too?"

She shrugged. "Maybe."

I wasn't going to get what I wanted from Patrice. If someone wanted Jett and me distracted, I would almost bet something was going down at the sheriff's office. I hurried out the door and hoped Brian would keep Patrice where she was.

When I got to the sheriff's office, I found Jane sitting at her desk.

"Hi, Jane. Do you know what's going on?"

"An old abandoned building caught fire."

"Do you mind if I stay here? I'm worried someone might come try something. I think the fire might be a distraction."

"That's fine."

"Can I go talk to the boys back there?"

"It's fine by me."

"Thanks." Once there was more office help, I wouldn't be able to get back here so easily. Jane was easygoing and probably not supposed to let just anyone back. I opened the door a crack, and I could hear Noah and Carlos arguing. I paused and listened.

"I don't see how you can think that none of this is your fault. It's all your fault," Noah was saying.

"What are you talking about?" Carlos asked.

"I know you planned this all and tried to pin it on me."

"Pin what on you? Where is this conversation even coming from?"

I stepped in. I could see both of them through the bars, but they couldn't see each other because there was a wall separating them.

"I think he heard the door open," I said. "He wanted whoever was coming in to think they were overhearing something important."

Noah walked over to the bars and held them in both his hands, and looked at me. "You're all getting this wrong. Carlos is the mastermind behind everything."

I shrugged. "Whether he is or not, you deserve to be here. You're the reason Deputy Ledford has a concussion, and you held us at gunpoint. Carlos wasn't there."

Carlos climbed off his bed and came closer. "Do you work with the police? I thought you just owned the diner?"

"She does," Noah said. "I asked around. She gets into people's business and drives the sheriff crazy."

Carlos frowned. "I'm pretty sure she's dating the sheriff."

I rolled my eyes. "That has nothing to do with this. I'm just trying to figure out what you are all up to so I can help Livy. She's my friend, and I think she's innocent."

"Her fingerprints were the only ones besides Jacob's on that EpiPen," Noah said. "That makes her look guilty to me."

"It might look that way," I said. "But Carlos and his friend broke into my place to plant more evidence on Livy. That makes her look innocent."

Carlos crossed his arms. "We weren't planting anything."

"Oh no? Multiple people searched through Livy's possessions before she arrived at my house. Now there's suddenly evidence? The sheriff knows it wasn't there before, and we know Carlos was there."

"Does that mean Carlos killed Jacob?" Noah asked.

"I didn't kill anyone!" Carlos protested. "I was just helping a friend. She said we would only be there for a minute, and there was something she needed. I panicked when the sheriff came in. All I did was help break in."

"Why are you protecting your friend? If what you're saying is true, why not tell who is behind it so you don't take the fall for them?"

Carlos's jaw went tight, and he sat on his bed. He wasn't talking anymore. I sighed. Working with this group was frustrating.

Chapter 17

"Can I leave a note on Sheriff Malone's desk?" I asked Jane before I left the sheriff's office.

"Sure," she said, not looking up from her computer. I was grateful, but a little concerned about Jane's lack of security. I went into Jett's office and studied it. Sending him a text would be more effective, but I wanted to see his office when he wasn't there. I frowned. I really was a snoopy person.

Everything was neat and organized. I wondered if Jett's mom had been coming in and cleaning it. I smiled when I thought about my last meeting with Carol Malone.

I moved over to the other side of his desk and grabbed a sticky note. I spotted a picture of me next to his computer and frowned. He must have taken it when I wasn't looking. I was in the diner mixing something in a bowl and wearing the ugly cat apron.

I heard someone talking to Jane, and I paused. I peeked out the crack in the door and saw Hannah.

"Can I please speak to Noah?" she asked.

Jane frowned. "Who are you?"

"His girlfriend."

"Sorry. You'll have to come back later when the sheriff is here," Jane said. I nodded. At least she wasn't letting just anyone in.

Hannah's mouth turned down, and she pulled a knife from her coat. "I didn't want it to come to this," she said. "I need you to unlock Noah and give me the keys to your car."

Jane's eyes narrowed. "I don't think so." I looked around Jett's office, but there wasn't anything I could easily grab. The pocket knife Boyd gave me was in my pocket, but it wasn't impressive for self-defense.

Hannah stepped closer to Jane's desk, but I could tell from her movements she was uncertain. Jane really should be behind some type of protective glass.

"The sheriff is busy with the fire," Hannah said. "He won't be back to help you until it's too late."

Jane shrugged. "What will you do if you kill me? I don't have the keys. You can't free anyone. All it will do is get you arrested for murder. There's a camera right there," she said, pointing at the corner. "You've already gotten yourself into plenty of trouble."

Hannah looked at the camera and grabbed a mug from Jane's desk. She flung it at the camera. I couldn't see the camera, but I heard the mug shatter.

Jane raised her brow. "That was a nice effort but a little low. Even if you break the camera, the feed is already saved. There's nothing you can do about that." I smiled. I was going to like Jane.

"Let him go!" Hannah yelled.

"I told you, I don't have the key."

"You're lying! They wouldn't leave the prisoners with no way out. What if there was an emergency?"

I grabbed the picture of me off Jett's desk. It was heavier than it looked. I flung the door open and chucked the picture with everything in me, aiming at Hannah's face. She shrieked and dropped the knife to cover her face.

I thought I moved fast, but before I could get to her, Jane had jumped over her desk and grabbed the knife. I kept going and plowed into Hannah, knocking her to the ground. She clawed at me, and I sat on her stomach and grabbed her arms, pushing them over her head and against the floor. Without a weapon, she wasn't a threat. She tried to kick me off her, but she couldn't get her legs up high enough.

"None of that," Jane said. "I have her legs." Peeking behind me, I saw Jane sitting on the girl's legs. I wasn't sure how long I could hold her like this. "The sheriff should be here any moment."

"Even with the fire going?" I asked.

"I hope so. I pushed the panic button. It goes directly to his phone, so if he looks at it, I think he'll come."

"Let me up!" Hannah yelled. She tried to spit on my face, but it fell back into her own.

I smiled. "That wasn't well thought out."

"This isn't my fault! It's all Carlos. He framed Noah."

"Noah did enough, even if that's true. And so have you." I was getting a cramp in my side, and my arms were shaking from holding her like this.

The door burst open, and Jett ran in. His eyes fixed on us and sparkled. He walked to us and helped Jane to her feet. He grabbed Hannah's wrists below where I had them. "Okay, Ivs. Let go and get off." I quickly got to my feet, and Jett pulled her up easily and shoved her arms behind her back.

"This isn't fair!" Hannah cried as he cuffed her.

"She came in with a knife," Jane said, pointing at the knife on her desk.

Jett nodded. "We don't have enough cells. I don't dare put any of these people together."

Jane grabbed a chair and pushed it over to a long pole that went from the ceiling to the floor in the corner. Jett dragged a protesting Hannah over and cuffed her to the pole and pushed her shoulders down so she was sitting on the chair.

I tilted my head. "I thought that was like a fireman pole that someone put in the wrong place," I said.

Jett grinned. "It's only a temporary fix, but I need to help get that fire under control. It's not an important building, but we don't want it spreading."

He looked from Hannah to Jane. "I hate to leave you with her, but I can't be in two places."

"I'm fine," Jane said, sitting at her desk. "I didn't even have to pull out my gun."

Jett looked at the picture frame on the floor and the broken mug and brown liquid on the wall and floor. "Alright, I'll try to hurry." He rushed out the door.

"You had a gun the entire time?" I asked.

Jane smiled. "I took this job because I became tired of too much drama. I used to work as a police officer in Topeka. That doesn't mean I've lost my touch, though."

"I thought you were new to all this since you keep letting me go talk to prisoners without screening me or anything."

"Nope. I'm new to the secretary stuff, but I'm still pretty tough. I've thoroughly researched you. You've had an interesting career since you came to Kansas."

"This is ridiculous!" Hannah said from her chair. "If you let me go, I can give you money. Please?"

"Don't add bribery to your crimes," I said.

Hannah's mouth turned down. "This is all Carlos's fault."

I crossed my arms. "I don't know why you keep trying to pin things on him. You and Noah have done plenty, and yours is even on video. I bet you started the fire as a diversion."

"Look," Hannah said. "I'll make a deal. I'll tell you everything if you let me go."

"Do we look stupid?" Jane asked.

Hannah slumped in her chair and covered her face with her hand.

"Can I guess?" I asked. I propped open the door to the cells and stood close. "Hey, Noah, we have Hannah in here."

"Hannah?" Noah called.

"Don't say anything!" Hannah yelled.

"You and Noah had a great plan," I said. "You get some friends together, form a little commune, and Noah goes around selling drugs. The people you recruit are people who are easily manipulated. Jacob joins, and he has a dominant personality. He begins taking over, and Noah loses some of his influence in the group."

Hannah looked up. "Jacob was a jerk, but everyone thought that. You can't blame anyone for hating him."

"Okay, so Jacob's ruining everything and being a jerk." I noticed she hadn't denied anything about the drugs. "He's going to ruin everything you've been working for. You're also annoyed because Noah is spending time with Livy. Noah has a habit of dumping you and taking you back. You can't have him falling for Livy. You kill Jacob and blame Livy. That should have solved both of your problems."

"Is that true, Hannah?" Noah called.

Hannah's lip trembled. "Of course not. I'm not a killer."

"You knew I was going to dump you for Livy," Noah said. "I bet the diner lady is right."

"What does Livy have that I don't?" Hannah sobbed.

"She's not crazy and jealous, for one thing. She doesn't fly into rages all the time."

"And she hated you! She never would have fallen for you!"

"I can't believe I let you pull me into this," Carlos said. "All I did was help Hannah break into the diner. I didn't know what was going on."

"I bet that's the same with Patrice," I said. "You used her to try to distract me when you set the fire so everyone would be preoccupied."

Hannah glared at me. "Good luck proving any of that. My father has a great lawyer."

"Your father won't even talk to you!" Noah called. "That's part of the reason all of this happened."

"He'll forgive me. He always does."

"Not this time. I'm not going down for murder," Noah said. "I'll admit to the drugs, but the murder is all you. I didn't know anything about that. Livy was guilty in my mind until now."

"Why drugs?" Jane asked. "You both come from wealthy families. I've looked into it."

"We both got cut off by our parents," Noah said. "I knew a guy who hooked me up with the drugs. He was telling me what to do."

"Don't admit anything!" Hannah sobbed.

"I'd rather go to prison for what I've done than for what you've done."

"I think I'm going to reevaluate my life," Carlos said. "And get some new friends."

"You dragged plenty of people into this. What about the others who were arrested after you held us at the cabin?" I asked Noah. "They still haven't talked, but they might once they realize you've all been arrested."

"They don't know anything," Hannah said. "All they were doing was trying to help Noah board up that cabin. They won't have anything to say against us."

Jane laughed. "I think you've said plenty. And all on video."

Hannah scowled. "If we're going down, I want everyone to go with us. Almost everyone at the camp knew about the drugs."

"I didn't," Carlos said. "And I doubt Livy did."

"Livy wasn't the type to trust with something like that," Hannah said. "She should still go down with us."

"Why?" I asked.

Hannah just frowned.

"You're the one who killed Jacob."

"You aren't going to prove it. Nothing had my prints, remember?"

"I'm not going down with you for killing Jacob," Noah said. "We're done forever, Hannah."

Her face turned red, and she clenched her fists. "You're lucky I can't get to you, Noah!" she yelled. "Everything I did was for us. I got rid of Jacob so you could have the life you wanted."

Jane pointed at the camera, and Hannah crossed her arms.

"I don't care about the camera. My father has connections. I won't spend any time in jail. I can say it out straight, and my father's lawyers will still get me out."

"Maybe if he takes your call," Noah said. I closed the door. I think we had enough evidence.

Chapter 18

My apartment smelled like popcorn when I entered. Livy and Boyd sat on the couch watching a movie. Livy looked tired and stressed, but she smiled when I entered.

"We heard the fire truck," Boyd said. "What's going on?"

"Hannah started a fire so she could try to get Noah out of jail."

Livy raised her brow. "That's crazy."

I smiled and sat on the arm of the couch. "She pretty much admitted to killing Jacob, so I think you can rest easy."

Livy grinned. "Really? That's such a relief. I'm going to go call my parents." She jumped up and went to her room.

Boyd held out the bowl of popcorn, and I grabbed a handful. "My leg is doing a lot better. I should probably think about moving in with Jett now that things will possibly calm down."

"Are you sure?"

"Yep. I'll try to rent out my house just in case I need it someday. Living alone is so—lonely."

"Do you think José will move in as well?" I asked.

"No idea. It makes him nervous. If he sells his house, then Jett decides to get married or something, then where would he be? José doesn't want to rent out his house because it's old and has problems. He doesn't want to do the landlord thing."

"That's a valid concern." I would ignore the married comment.

"Of course, Jett said he's not attached to the house, and he'd rather live in your apartment, so it's probably not something we have to worry about. When you get married, one of us could buy Jett's house."

I laughed. "Married? I don't see that happening soon."

My phone rang, and I went to the kitchen to take it. "Hello?"

"Hey," Jett said. "I'm taking some of the corn kids to Wichita in a few minutes. Jane showed me the video. I think it will be a pretty easy case to close."

"Oh good. I bet Livy's going to go home."

"That's good. I bet she's relieved."

"The two girls at the movie with Hannah admitted she made them lie for her. They said she only came at the very end."

"That's what I figured. How long will you be?"

"I'm not sure, but I'll be smiling the entire way there."

"Why?"

"I can't get the image out of my head of you and Jane holding Hannah down. You looked like you might bite someone, and Jane just sat on Hannah's legs in her pantsuit, looking like she was about to sip her tea."

I smiled. "I wish I'd seen it."

"I'll never forget it. I'll talk to you later, alright?"

"Okay. Bye."

"Bye."

The mayor's party was bigger than I'd expected. He was hosting people to talk about reelecting him. The party room was full, and all the cooks were working at top speed. Even though Livy had been cleared, the mayor hadn't apologized for making us lose days' worth of wages.

I took platters of desserts into the room and placed them around different tables. The mayor stood at the head of the room, talking about everything he would do if he were reelected. I couldn't help wondering why he hadn't done any of them before.

A man I didn't know stood. "What about all the crime we've had recently? What are you going to do about that?"

"I'm hoping we elect a new sheriff," the mayor said, causing me to pause and glare at him. "Deputy Ledford will be running, and I think he'll make a difference."

"Ledford's not going to get elected," someone else said. "It's not Sheriff Malone's fault all this stuff has happened. He's dealt with all of it."

Mayor Jepson looked at me. "He doesn't always use the correct channels. He allows people who aren't qualified to help him."

I crossed my arms but forced myself to stay silent.

"If he gets things done, why do you care?" the man said. "We don't need a new sheriff. The sheriff needs more help. What can we do about that?"

I grabbed an empty platter and left the room before I did something regrettable. There had to be a better person to run for mayor.

The servers were all running around trying to serve all the people in the dining area, so when Ledford came in, I went and greeted him.

"Hello, Deputy Ledford. How are you?"

He shrugged and took off his hat. "I've been better, but I've been worse."

"Let me get you a table." I led him to an empty booth. "What can I get you?"

He sighed. "Can we talk?"

Ledford was one of the last people in town I wanted to talk to, but I sat down and waited. He stared down at his hat and didn't say anything.

"What is it?" I finally asked.

He looked up. "I hate it when you stick your nose into things. You don't listen, and you're going to get in trouble someday."

"Probably."

"I do want to thank you, though. If you weren't the way you are, there's no telling what would have happened to me in that cabin. Of course, if you hadn't snuck in and told me about the cabin, I wouldn't have been there in the first place."

I should have known he was still going to blame me.

"But if you hadn't gone, we wouldn't have known about the drugs, and Noah probably would have gotten away because no one would have checked on him. I guess I'm saying thank you, but try to stay out of things from now on. I know Jett lets you do what you want, but it needs to stop."

"I'm not promising anything."

"I hope you'll consider getting a hobby. You aren't trained, and things won't end well one day for you. You can only be lucky so many times."

I just looked at him. I wasn't sure what to say.

"I'll have a cheeseburger, medium rare."

I nodded and stood.

He smiled. "I'd prefer it if it didn't end up on my lap this time."

I remembered back to the time I'd dumped his food on his lap and smiled. "I can probably arrange that."

"The mayor should have warned us better," José said when I got to the kitchen. "He should have had people pre-order so we could do this smoother."

"We'll make it," Carrie said. "So long as we don't get anyone complaining and sending things back."

"That doesn't happen often, does it?" I asked.

José shook his head. "Nah, but the mayor has been known to do it. He does it often, actually."

"Ledford just thanked me for saving him," I said. "I never thought I would see that day,"

"Maybe there's hope for him after all," Carrie said. "I wouldn't bet on it, though."

Chapter 19

Boyd wasn't a hoarder like Barbra, but he still had a lot of stuff. We'd been moving him into Jett's house for two days. We were taking a lot of it to donate, but it was taking a long time. We'd had to pack it all as well since Boyd's leg was still sore. He'd bossed us around while we packed, but now we were moving it all while he was waiting at the diner.

"When Boyd dies, I'm going to have to get all this stuff out of my basement," Jett said as he carried a big box into his house.

I smiled. "It's about noon. Do you want me to run to the diner and bring back lunch?"

"Why don't we take a break and eat?"

"Okay."

He took my hand, and we walked toward the diner.

When we got close, I saw a man with a cowboy hat standing near the library. I'd seen him before. He was the man who had handed Noah a backpack before I knew anything was going on. He was standing, looking at his watch.

"Do you know that man?" I asked.

"No," Jett said. "He must be passing through."

"I've seen him before. He gave Noah a backpack, then hurried away when I saw him."

"Interesting. Do you mind if we talk to him for a minute?"

"That's fine." We walked toward him, and the man shifted nervously. He had another backpack over his arm.

"Hello," Jett said, holding out his hand. The man shook it. "I'm Sheriff Malone. Are you new to town?"

"No," the man said, clutching the bag. "I'm just meeting my nephew here."

"Oh? Who is he? I think I know everyone in town."

The man shifted again. "He's new, so you probably haven't met. He should be here," he said, looking around.

"I've seen you before," I said. "You were with Noah. Is he your nephew?"

"Oh... yes."

"He's not here anymore," Jett said.

"Where is he?"

"Jail."

The man's eyes went wide. "Oh. Then I better be getting on."

"He was dealing drugs."

The man coughed. "That's unexpected."

"Is it?" Jett asked, taking a step closer. The man turned and ran. "Stop!" Jett sighed. "I'll be back." He took off after the man and caught him quickly, knocking him to the ground. The backpack fell to the ground.

"Those aren't mine!" the man said, pointing at the backpack. "I was just holding them for Noah."

I picked up the bag and looked inside. It was full of baggies of white powder, just like before. "It's full of drugs," I confirmed.

Jett muttered something as he cuffed the man. "Can't I have one day when nothing happens?"

I smiled and handed him the bag. "I'll meet you at the diner."

He nodded and led the man away.

I found Boyd sitting in a booth, eating a piece of pie. I sat across from him.

"Where's Jett?" he asked.

"I think we found the guy who was getting drugs to Noah. Jett's taking him in."

"Poor Jett. That guy needs a break."

"It sounds like he's getting more help."

"Yep. That will be nice for everyone. How's Ledford?"

"It sounds like he's doing better. His doctor won't sign that he can return to work yet, so he must still have some healing."

I ordered food for Jett and me, guessing what he would want. He was a big burger fan, so I figured that was safe. When he came in and spotted us, he waved. Sinking on the bench next to me, he sighed.

"How much junk can one person have, Boyd?"

Boyd laughed. "A lot."

"I think we're getting close. You should hire someone to go deep clean your house before you get renters in there."

Boyd nodded. "I was planning on it."

"I got a call when I was walking here. Three deputies have been hired. Between them and Ledford, we should be a lot better off."

"Nice," I said, sipping my water. It felt strange sitting in here like I was a customer.

"It's more than nice. Do you realize what that means? If five of us take twelve-hour shifts, I'll have time where I'm not on duty or on call." He placed his arm over my shoulder. "That means we can actually go on dates that aren't crime scenes."

I smiled. "What will that be like?"

"It'll be great. Two of them are coming tomorrow. I figure they might as well start right away. If anyone needs me in two days, I'll be at the pool."

I raised my brow. "The pool? In Wichita?"

"No. At the B&B."

"They have a pool?"

Boyd chuckled. "They have a pool and a hot tub. They overcharge something fierce, but it's nice. No lifeguards on duty, so you have to sign a bunch of waivers."

"Did Livy go home?" Jett asked.

"Yes. Her parents probably won't let her leave again. She said she got a half-hour lecture. She's going to come back and work here until she decides what she wants to do."

Boyd scratched his head. "She was always the best server. She never forgets the straw."

"And that's the most important thing?" I asked.

"Yes. Drinking soda from a straw just tastes better."

⚜

We had Boyd moved in by dinner, and I was back at the diner. I didn't have anything to do, so I washed the dishes. Livy came in the back door and motioned to me. I followed her back outside into the cool evening air.

"Is something wrong?" I asked.

"No. I just... I want to talk to Anton, but I don't know what to say."

I bit my lip. "I'm not good at that type of thing."

"But you have Jett."

"That just happened."

She sighed. "I can't sit around waiting for him to do something. He might not feel like I do, but I have to know. It could change what I want to do in the future."

"I guess you could just outright ask him how he feels. It might be awkward and might not go how you want it to, but at least you'll know."

Her eyes showed worry, but she nodded. We went back into the kitchen, and she took a deep breath and walked to where Anton was whisking something.

He looked up when she came near and smiled. "Hey, Liv. I'm glad things worked out for you."

"Thanks."

"Ivy said you're going to be working here again."

"Yes." She fiddled with her hands. I wondered if she would dare to ask if they could talk. She looked more likely to run. "Can I ask you something?"

He grinned. "Sure."

I cringed. Wasn't she going to at least take him outside? Carrie and José were both here, and I could tell they were pretending not to listen.

"I'm trying to decide what I want to do with my life."

"Yeah, that's a hard one. I sometimes wonder if I'll ever know what I want to do." He kept whisking his mixture.

I could see her hands shaking. "I was just wondering if, um, well, ugh." She covered her face with her hands.

Anton frowned. "What's wrong?"

She put her arms down and took another deep breath. "Do you think there might ever be anything between us?"

Anton dropped his whisk on the floor, and his mouth hung open. "Between you and me?" he said, a little high-pitched.

Carrie and I shared a smile.

Livy nodded.

Anton swallowed and blinked a few times. "Do you want there to be?"

José smacked himself in the head.

Anton took a step toward her. "Because I've hoped since I first met you."

Livy put a hand to her heart. "Really?"

"Really." They both stood there, staring at each other.

José crossed his arms. "So kiss her already."

Carrie frowned. "Isn't that skipping some steps?"

"I'd really like to skip those steps," Livy said.

José snorted, and I shot him a look.

Anton grinned. "Can we go outside?" He grabbed Livy's hand, and they rushed out the back door.

"That was so awkward and cute!" Carrie gushed.

"I thought I was going to have to give them instructions." José turned back to his cooking. "I guess if Ivy and Jett can figure it out, there's hope for everyone."

"Ha ha," I said. "Who are you to talk? When's the last time you went on a date?"

José shook his head. "I would if I had someone I wanted to date."

Carrie frowned and went to the fridge.

"Besides, once a guy gets to be my age and isn't married, there's usually something wrong with him."

"So what's wrong with you?"

"I work too much. No woman wants that."

"You do work too much. You can have more time off."

"Not all women mind a workaholic," Carrie said, pulling butter from the fridge.

José watched Carrie peel off the wrapper, and his eyes narrowed. "No one wants a workaholic. Relationships need time. That's something I don't have."

"That's stupid."

I raised my brows and wondered if I should leave.

"What's stupid?" José asked.

"Not making time for anything important." Carrie tossed the butter in a pan and frowned. She handed the pan to José. "I need to leave. I have a headache." She took off her apron, tossed it in the dirty clothes basket, and walked to the back door.

"Wait!" I said. "Livy and Anton." She turned and went out through the front.

José frowned at the pan. "What am I supposed to do with this?"

I giggled. "I don't know."

"Why are you giggling like that?"

"You have Carrie so upset she didn't even know what she was doing."

"Why is she upset? Because I said I work a lot?"

"Too much for a relationship?"

He pulled at his hairnet. "Why would she—no. Stop looking at me like that."

I giggled again. "You're as clueless as Anton."

"Carrie doesn't—like me, does she?"

I shrugged. "I don't know, but it looks like she might."

José shoved the pan in my hands. "I'll be back. I need to go in my office and think for a minute." He disappeared behind a door.

I looked down at the pan of butter, then at the dirty whisk on the floor, and smiled.

Chapter 20

"The snow is melting," I told Creepers two days later. "Soon, we might only need jackets. Well, I guess you always have a coat." Things were picking up at the diner, and I could feel spring in the air.

I hadn't seen Jett in a couple of days. He'd spent yesterday taking the new deputies around, getting them acquainted with the town. José said they'd come in for dinner, but I hadn't been around. I got a text from Jett saying he was at the pool and I could come if I wanted.

Swimming had never been my favorite thing, so I didn't even have a swimming suit. I decided to go over anyway just to say hello. I'd hoped Jett would want to spend his first day off with me and not Boyd.

I grabbed my jacket and made my way to the B&B. Jett deserved downtime. He was going to have even more trials now that all this stuff had happened, so he might as well make the most of his free time.

I went into the B&B and wandered around until I found a glass door. I could see a pool, so I went in. A hot tub was off to the side, and Jett sat inside. Jett rested his arms on the concrete behind him and wore his sunglasses. There were big windows with light shining in, but not enough to need sunglasses.

I grinned as I walked up to him. "What are you doing?"

"It's my day off, baby," Jett said.

"What's with the sunglasses?"

"It just fits the mood."

I arched my eyebrow. "Hmm. It's a little weird when you're inside."

"Hey, you relax your way, and I'll relax mine."

I sat by him.

"Aren't you getting in?"

"Nope. I don't even own a swimming suit."

"Did José talk to you about the competition?"

"What competition?"

"I probably shouldn't tell you. It's José's thing."

I pulled Jett's sunglasses off and put them next to me. "I kind of thought we would do something on your day off."

"That's why I told you to come here. You should go buy a swimming suit."

"I seriously doubt I'd be able to find one this time of year."

"You're probably right." Before I had time to prepare, Jett grabbed me and dropped me into the middle of the hot tub. I screamed and landed on my feet and managed to keep the upper part of me dry. I stood there glaring at him.

"Now what?" I asked, putting my hands on my hips. "I'm going to have to walk home like this. I'm going to freeze."

He grinned. "I doubt you'll freeze. It's like fifty-five degrees out there."

"Miss Medley already hates me." I stepped out of the hot water onto the concrete and immediately shivered.

"My towel is over there," he said, pointing.

I grabbed his towel and wrapped it around myself. "Have fun walking home like that." I began hurrying to the door.

Jett caught up with me and grabbed my arms. "You're really going to make me walk home wet?"

"Yep. You brought this on yourself." I went on my toes and kissed him lightly. "I'll go change and bring you a dry towel even though you don't deserve it."

He smiled. "I'll be in the water. Thanks."

I dripped across the B&B but managed to avoid seeing Miss Medley. It was cold outside, but I got home quickly. It only took a minute to change and grab a pink towel. There were other colors, but I thought Jett deserved pink. I had a text from José asking me to come talk to him. I stopped in the diner kitchen.

"Hey, José."

He turned from the salad he was creating and smiled. "Have you ever heard of The Culinary Roadshow?"

"No."

"It's really hard to get into. It's a huge baking competition. The winning team gets a cash prize plus the right to brag. It's even broadcast on YouTube. It has a big following even though the filming and everything is a bit amateurish. Getting approved isn't easy because there are only three groups from different small restaurants. I entered Sue's Diner, and we got in."

"When is it?"

"It's in about a month. I didn't tell you because I didn't think we would get in. I thought you might want to go for some publicity. Oh, and most of it takes place on a train. The train stops in different cities for each round. It goes from LA to Chicago."

"That might be fun."

"We can take up to four people. I think we should take Boyd and Jett. They could both use a change of scenery."

"What about the diner?" I asked.

"Carrie and Anton can handle it. I'm sure they would do it if we gave them a bonus. They would be more helpful than Boyd and Jett, but someone needs to keep an eye on things here."

"And Jett knows about this?"

"Yep. He's excited."

"I guess it might be fun. Except the TV part."

"We will have to let Jett and Boyd bake, though. Everyone on the team has to help."

"Have you ever seen Jett bake?"

"Nope. We'll just tell them what to do. It will be a nice break for everyone."

"Sounds good. I need to go, but I'll be back in a few minutes." I rushed from the kitchen and almost ran into two men wearing clothing similar to Jett's sheriff outfit. "Sorry," I said.

They were both tall. The one with curly brown hair stepped back. "Are you Sheriff Malone's girlfriend?"

My stomach fluttered at the thought of being called Jett's girlfriend. "Yes."

"We ate here last night. It's a nice place you have. The sheriff told us it was great, and we weren't disappointed."

"Thank you." They nodded, and I hurried back to the B&B. I already liked those deputies better than Ledford.

I entered the building and saw Miss Medley mopping where I'd dripped. I tried not to look guilty as I hurried back to Jett. He had his sunglasses on again.

"No one looks cool wearing sunglasses inside," I informed him.

He grinned and tipped them down. "It makes me feel invisible."

196

"Do you want to be invisible?"

"Sometimes." He stood, and I handed him the towel. "Nice color."

"José told me about the competition."

He put the towel over his shoulders. "And we're going to do it, right?"

"Yeah, it might be fun. I've never ridden a train."

"I got the new deputies just in time. I'm supposed to have about thirty days off a year, but I've never gotten to take more than a few."

"It will be nice to have a vacation with no stress."

Jett grinned. "Trouble seems to follow you. I wouldn't count on it."

"Follows me? I think it's been just as close to you."

He winked. "True. It didn't happen until you came, though. Riding a train to a baking competition sounds harmless enough."

I smiled. "What could possibly go wrong?"

Fluffy Pancakes

2 cups all-purpose flour

¼ cup sugar

1 tablespoon baking powder

2 teaspoons baking soda

1 teaspoon salt

2 cups buttermilk

½ cup plus 2 tablespoons vegetable oil

2 large eggs

Instructions

1. **Prepare the Dry Ingredients**:
   In a large mixing bowl, whisk together the flour, sugar, baking powder, baking soda, and salt until well combined.

2. **Mix the Wet Ingredients**:
   In a separate bowl, whisk together the buttermilk, oil, and eggs until smooth.

3. **Combine and Rest**:
   Gradually pour the wet ingredients into the dry ingredients, stirring gently until just combined. Be careful not to overmix—the batter should be slightly lumpy. Let the batter rest for 20 minutes. This step is crucial for fluffy pancakes, so don't skip it!

4. **Heat the Skillet**:

Place a skillet or griddle over medium-high heat and let it warm up until hot. Lightly oil the surface to prevent sticking.

5. **Cook the Pancakes**:

Scoop ¼ cup of batter for each pancake and pour onto the hot skillet. Cook until the edges are set, the bottom is golden brown, and bubbles form on the surface, about 2–3 minutes. Flip and cook for another 1–2 minutes until golden on both sides.

6. **Serve and Enjoy**:

Transfer the pancakes to a plate and serve immediately with warm syrup or your favorite toppings. Makes about four servings.

Also By Kristy Dixon

<u>Cozy Mystery</u>
Murder With a Side of Bacon
Murder With a Hint of Cinnamon
Murder With a Fudge Brownie to Go
Murder With a Splash of Vanilla

<u>Young Adult</u>
Akkron (The Silver Eclipse Book 1)
Boztoll (The Silver Eclipse Book 2)
The Other Continent (The Silver Eclipse Book 3)
The Amethyst Crown

More Than Once Upon a Time
Trapped In Once Upon a Timen
The Beginning of Once Upon a Time
Blade of the Phoenix (Riviand Lost Book 1)
Mermaid's Demise (Riviand Lost Book 2)
Dragon's Cove (Riviand Lost Book 3)

<u>Coming Soon!</u>
Murder With a Slice of Pie

About the Author

Kristy Dixon started writing stories when she was seven and never stopped. She enjoys writing cozy mysteries and YA. At home, she spends her time playing board games with her husband and kids and writing. Occasionally she takes part in a Super Mario marathon. She has six chickens and a cat that help keep life amusing. If she isn't playing with her kids or writing, she is usually eating cookies, or wishing she was eating cookies.